Dmitri's Darling

Kinks & Conundrums Book 3

Anna Sparrows

Cover Design by Ky at Blue Brolli Graphics

*For my friends, even the ones who have no idea what my pen name is.
Thank you all for your support these last few months. It's been a wild
ride, and I wouldn't have survived without you all.
Sorry not sorry for all the cringeworthy Christmas puns.*

Preface

Dmitri's Darling is a ridiculously sweet, incredibly silly Christmas-themed Daddy kink novella **without** age play/age regression.

I openly admit that I did next to no research on the adult film industry when I wrote this, so you may want to invest deeply in your suspension of disbelief for this one. Instead, you're about to be submersed in a 22,000 word excuse to squeeze in as many puns as I possibly could.

As for warnings, there's some mild embarrassment, use of a gag, spanking, and a mild (non-graphic) on-page injury.

Oh, and did I mention the abundance of silly jokes?

Acknowledgements

Firstly, thank you to Anna, Jamie Lee, and Marianne at the *Daddy Kink and Age Gap MM books* group on Facebook. This novella is originally being published as part of the *DKAG Christmas Daddies Season Two* series, in celebration of the Facebook group, which is one of my favourite online spaces. Thank you for including me in this series, and for all your support over the years.

Secondly, thanks to my wonderful alpha and beta readers, Erin, Lauren, Megan, and Cindy. This book would not have happened if not for you.

Also, a huge thank you to my wonderful PA, Ky, for designing the *Kinks & Conundrums* cover. Similarly, thank you to Fantasia Frog Designs for the *DKAG Christmas Daddies Season Two* ebook cover!

Finally, thank you for picking this book up/clicking on the ebook. Your support is what keeps me writing.

Contents

Chapter One

Am I in the right place?

Standing in front of the director for this production, I frown. This is my first time auditioning for a film, but I always imagined these kinds of things happening in bland offices and not in the middle of fully decorated sets.

Right now, the space I'm in has been set up to look like a studio apartment at Christmastime. There's a bed with crisp white sheets, stockings hung under the fake windowsill, which is also dusted with fake snow on the other side of the plexiglass panes, and a forest-like setting taped on the same surface, giving the illusion of a pretty setting beyond these flimsy walls. In the corner of the room, there's a beautiful Christmas tree, lit up with twinkling lights and glinting baubles. Then, just down the wall from that, there's a door.

A handful of people bustle around outside the scene's walls, but fewer than I would have imagined for a movie set.

Maybe their lead dropped out at the last second, I realize slowly. That would make sense as to why I'm auditioning on set like this.

Positioned between the bed and the camera, I cock my head. "Where's the script?"

"Script?"

I feel like such a noob. Shuffling my feet, I reply, "Yeah, you know...the words you want me to say when I'm on screen?"

The director, who introduced himself to me as Jake, seems equally confused. "We...uh...we don't do scripts here. You just go with what you feel and if it isn't working, we will stop filming and redirect."

That...is odd.

"Oh." I blink. "So...improv. Is there, like, a vibe you want me to go for...?"

He snorts and sets aside his clipboard, waving his hands in the air as he says, "Dude, when Santa knocks on the door, be cute. If you're really feeling it, maybe crack a joke about being naughty or nice or something before you blow him, I don't know. Just go with it."

Did...did he just say...?

"Sorry, did you just—"

"Go pick out a costume." He cuts me off, sounding impatient now. He points over to a rack of clothing. "Anything from the rack grabbing your attention?"

Biting my lip, I meander across the small space and look over my options, then grin at the olden-timey long johns with the button-held butt-flap. It's made of red terry-toweling material, and it will probably be a bit snug, but it sings to my inner Boy. The woman who seems to be in charge of costumes, hair, and makeup (this must be a super low-budget project), pulls it from the rack.

"Let's get you into this now."

Wait. What? That's also kind of weird for an audition, isn't it? I open my mouth to question it, but she huffs and insists, "Now, please. We're burning daylight."

"Are we filming today?" I ask, tugging my socks and shoes off, hopping around on one foot and then the other. "My agent didn't mention—"

The woman gives me a strange look, the messy bun on her head wobbling almost precariously, like one vigorous nod might unravel the whole thing. "Yeah..." she replies slowly, then tilts her head. "What kind of shoots do you usually do?"

"Oh," I blush, "I've done a couple of ads, mostly print, but nothing like this." This is my first ever movie audition, and I am so excited for it, but I am trying to be professional.

Understanding seems to dawn over her. "Oh, you're a porn virgin," she says, then holds out the costume, "that explains a lot. Underwear off too, please."

Porn...virgin? Is that some kind of industry lingo I'm not familiar with?

Distracted, I get completely naked. "Sorry, what do you mean by—"

"He dressed yet?" the director snaps.

"Ten seconds," the costume lady calls back over her shoulder. She holds the onesie open for me to step into, seemingly unphased by my dick and balls being right in front of her. I guess she sees naked bodies all the time in her line of work. Nevertheless, I blush at her proximity.

"I don't...I don't even know my character's name," I admit, and she blinks in surprise.

"I don't think he really has a name."

Oh. My hopes sink a little. I thought I was auditioning for the romantic lead, but it must just be a side character. Swallowing roughly, I try to muster some cheer. "Well, that takes the pressure off."

She helps tug the long-johns up and wrangles my (admittedly large) biceps into the stretchy sleeves, furrows creating deep lines between her manicured eyebrows. The zip goes up, and I feel super exposed in this slutty (there's no other word for it) outfit.

Stepping back, she takes me in and the frown melts away, replaced by a satisfied smile. "Perfect."

"Excellent," Jake huffs, giving me a brief once over. He waves towards a table behind him. "Contracts are back there. Standard stuff. Make sure your stage name is clear and written in the right spot, unless you want your legal name credited."

"Stage name?" I ask, but he's already turned around to bark orders at the camera guy.

I head over to the table with the paperwork and pick up a blank copy. My jaw drops as I read some of the information about sex scenes and...why are they asking about my hard limits? Do they mean for stunts and shit? On a low budget Christmas romance?

This almost looks like one of the contracts I'd fill out at The Grove when I'm negotiating a scene with a Dom, but maybe I'm just so sex starved that I'm seeing things that aren't there. Maybe this is just a generic contract they use for everything.

I fill in my details, leaving the hard limits page blank to come back to, and flag down one of the two assistants in the room, handing it to them for them to check it.

They brush back bright blue bangs from their eyes and scan the document, snorting at my name in the Stage Name box. "This is your legal name, dude," they mutter. "Bit vanilla, isn't it? And you're brave for inviting the weirdos who watch this shit to find you so easily."

"Weirdos?" I mean, okay, tacky Christmas romances do tend to invite a certain kind of audience, but I think it's a bit cruel to call the people who enjoy them names.

"This is your first time, right?" The assistant asks, ignoring my question. I nod and they reach for the pen, leaning over the table as they cross out my name and replace it with—

"Miles Deep?" I gape at the page. That sounds kind of...*porny*. Like a bad pun about how good I am at bottoming, or something. And, okay, I *am* a good bottom, but...what the fuck is happening right now?

"Sounds *way* cooler than" —they check the paperwork and scrunch up their nose— "Miles Jeffries."

Excuse you, what's wrong with my name?

Despite having the protest on the tip of my tongue, I keep quiet. It's only a bit part. I can use my real name later, right? For bigger, better projects.

"You like it?" They prod, smiling hopefully. The piercing in their nose glints under the bright lighting above us. "I've always wanted to name a porn star." I can feel my eyes widening as realization begins to dawn, but they are already flipping through the contract again. "Hey, you've left your hard limits out. Seriously, you need to put them down or these guys might make you do things you're not comfortable with."

Like porn?!

I open my mouth to say those exact words, to explain that there's been a mix up and I have somehow found myself in the wrong place. That I was supposed to be auditioning for a low-budget, tacky Christmas romance movie, not a mid-budget tacky Christmas porn shoot. But then the assistant says, "I know that a grand for a scene might make some people want to stretch their limits, but you've already got this in the bag, so stick to your guns and don't do anything you don't want to do."

A grand? One thousand *dollars? For one scene?* And *I get to orgasm?*

I think of the repairs I need to make on my car. Of the phone bill I'm overdue to pay. A grand would cover both and leave me with enough money to cover half of a week's rent, too.

"Miles Deep is a great name," I agree, reaching for the pen and paper. Really, how different could this be to doing a scene in a club, except for the audience...and the camera...and the costumes? I scribble my limits —no heavy pain play or impact play, no CNC, no scat play (watersports okay)— and tick the box that says I have tested negative within the last month and that I am comfortable working without condoms. Satisfied with that, I hand the paperwork back, pulling out my phone to show proof of my last test results, which I only received a week ago. The assistant scribbles a note to say they've sighted them, then stashes the documents in a manilla envelope.

A thrill of anxious excitement travels up my spine, and I clap my hands together, bouncing on my heels. "So...when does Santa come?"

The assistant smirks. "Oh, just before Jake yells 'cut', I suppose."

I definitely walked right into that one.

Chapter Two

"**I**t's beginning to look a lot like *fuck this*," I sing to myself as I drive towards today's shoot. It's still October, but I'm all signed up to play Santa in a Christmas-themed scene with some newbie.

It'll be just my luck that he's got no stamina or freaks out about the cameras and bails like the last one did.

Or, my inner voice grumbles, *says he only does scenes with buff guys.*

I still haven't gotten over the sting of that particular interaction.

I'm a cuddly bear and proud of it, but sometimes I do consider whether I might get more work if I hit the gym and turn the keg I'm carrying into a six-pack.

But *ugh*, who wants to work out that much? Besides, my arms and ass get me plenty of work...and plenty of attention at The Grove, besides.

I just hope this newbie is professional.

Because that's the thing: it's porn. My scene partners don't have to be attracted to me, they just have to be able to fake it. Imagine some buff dude with abs for days if that's what you need to do to get off during the scene, I don't care. But don't whine like a bitch because they paired you with a bear instead of a gym bunny.

God, maybe I need to take a break from this shit. It's clearly starting to wear on me, which is kind of sad. I love what I do and have zero shame telling people I am an adult entertainer. My job makes people happy, or fills a void (no sex puns, please, I'm being serious), or even inspires people to spice things up a little. I love knowing that I'm playing a part in that. And, yeah, I do have some fun while I'm at it.

But as I've been aging, trends have changed. People have started wanting more of the fantasy and less reality from their porn stars. Sure, a niche market exists for all shapes and sizes, but I can't deny that I'm booking less work than I was a decade ago. And now I've hit an all-time low, playing porny Santa.

Ho, ho, fucking ho.

I've built up a comfortable nest-egg over the years, depositing most of my earnings into high-interest savings accounts and stock investments. It wouldn't hurt me to start stepping out of the industry. To leave while goings are good, with my head held high.

Leave 'em wanting more.

The old showbiz mantra makes me sigh as it slowly seeps through my musings like molasses.

What if I still want more, though?

Honestly, while I'm not sure that I really do, I think I'm clinging to this work because it's familiar, and I am good at it. I'm afraid of being fifty and adrift without purpose.

Maybe I could direct or produce my own shoots, I decide as I guide my car into a spare space on the familiar lot. *Or take up photography. Or...who the fuck knows?*

"Get out of your head," I mutter, staring my own eyes down in the rearview mirror. "You're not dead or irrelevant."

Just relegated to playing Santa. Ugh.

I grab my duffel from the passenger seat and drag my ass out of the car, affecting a confident swagger and a cocky grin as I make my way to today's studio. The fact that we're shooting in an actual studio and not some cheap motel room does bode well for the quality of the production, at least.

Sonya greets me at the studio door and nabs my bag, pulling me in for a hug with over-the-top air kisses to each of my cheeks. "Dimmy, I've missed you," she declares, tossing my bag onto a nearby makeup chair and hustling me over to the costumes. Already tugging my shirt over my head like the whirlwind she is, she says, "Your co-star for this one is a cutie."

"Oh?" I ask, as if Jake hasn't already texted to tell me he'd just cast a 'hot newbie' who was 'ten thousand percent your type'.

She's grabbed a thin pair of red pull-apart sweats and she nods. "He seemed a bit confused and...I don't know...uncertain, I guess? At least, he did at first. But then he had a chat with Jamie, of all people, and has been practically bouncing around the set like a golden retriever."

I fight the urge to groan. Unhinged enthusiasm doesn't always translate to performing well on camera. Casting my gaze around the room, I try to spy the new guy, but everyone else is familiar to me. "And where is our new puppy, then?"

"Had to go to the little boy's room," she answers easily, pulling the pants up my legs and settling the waistband low on my hips. My bare belly overhangs it anyway. Sonya grabs the matching thin red jacket with white trim and helps me ease my arms into it, but she leaves the ensemble undone, stepping back to inspect her handiwork with a nod to herself. "Jake's not gonna throw you into a scene with each other without a little meet and greet first, though."

I nod. It's unusual —but not entirely unheard of at some of the lower-budget productions— to just shove a couple of entertainers in a room and see what they come up with. I personally like to talk through my plans for the scene, assuming nothing specific has been requested by the director, to make sure my scene partner is comfortable with it all. It's all well and good to be handed a dossier with a list of hard and soft limits, but I get a better feel for what my scene partner will most enjoy by talking it out and seeing their reactions. It's really not all that different from indulging at my local kink club, only when I am there, I am there for my own needs and entertainment.

"Here's your hat, Santa," she winks and hands the item over, then raises her chin, gesturing behind me, "and here's your Boy."

I paste on a warm smile and turn to greet my co-star, then almost swallow my tongue.

Rudolph's right testicle, he's gorgeous.

And familiar.

Why is he familiar?

"Oh," the muscular man, whose body is testing the limits of the stretchy red long-johns he's wearing, practically inhales the word. He sounds —and looks— bashful, a pink flush dusting his clean-shaven cheeks. "Um, hi."

"Hi," I reply, a little dumbly. Licking my lips and ignoring Sonya's rapt attention at our awkward introduction, I ask, "have we met?"

His cheeks turn even more pink, and he shakes his head. "Not...not officially, no. I—"

Oh. Maybe he's a fan.

"You've...seen my work?" I offer gently, though that doesn't explain why he's familiar to me. Not unless he's been stalking me or something.

Clearing his throat, he says, "No. I, um, I didn't know you were...I mean, not that there's anything wrong with...because I'm here, too, right? But...no, I...no." He winces, scrunching his nose up adorably before he sighs and says, "The club. I've, um, I've seen you around...*the club*." He raises his eyebrows pointedly and I have to bite back a chuckle.

Subtle, this guy is not.

It's cute.

The club he's talking about is, of course, The Grove. It's our city's premiere kink club. Exclusive, expensive, and breaking the iron-clad NDAs will get you kicked out instantly. Already interested in this guy, I perk up even more at the knowledge that he's obviously a regular at my kink club, which means he's gotta be kinky himself. And, if his demeanor is anything to go by at a glance, he's gotta be a sub of some kind.

My catnip.

Allowing a slow, sly smirk to curl my lips, I nod and look him over from head to toe and then back again. He squirms a little under my appraisal, but does his best to stay still. *That* dings all my bells. As does the impossible-to-conceal growing bulge at his crotch.

"So, you know me," I practically purr at him, delighting in the flush crawling up his neck, "but I don't know you. Why don't we sit and get to know each other a little before the cameras start rolling?"

Chapter Three

Of course he's a porn star, I muse as I try to gather my wits about me.

Dmitri is kind of a legend at The Grove. One of those doms all of us subs and switches would sell our souls to do a single scene with. Not only because he is hotter than the sun —which he definitely is, with his shaggy beard, undercut hair, and intricate tattoos all over those massive arms— but also because he's known for his exceptional attention to detail and aftercare.

The Grove, being the exclusive establishment that it is, is known to have a high calibre of patrons to start with, but Master Dmitri is the cream of the crop.

And I'm about to have sex with him.

On camera.

I am so fucked, and not in the way I want to be...though I guess that will happen as well. If I can make it that far.

I've got the *hugest* crush on this Dom and it's been a while since I've had another person's hands on me, so...

This is going to be the shortest porn scene ever.

I'm already getting hard just from *looking* at him. I'll come the second he touches me, I just know it.

As Dmitri leads me over to the table where I'd signed my contract, I try to formulate words that aren't 'fuck' and 'me'. My mouth is dry and my thoughts are spinning. The fact that his Sexy Santa costume leaves very little to my imagination isn't helping me.

"So, how long have you been going to The Grove?" he asks as he pulls up one of the folding chairs and spins it with a casual ease that makes my stomach swoop. I stifle a groan when he sits on it backwards, powerful thighs straddling either side of the metal frame of the chair's backing.

Lucky fucking chair.

No...wait. I'll *be* the chair soon enough.

God help me, I might just come in my onesie untouched at this point.

Hang on, did he just ask a question? He did, didn't he? *Focus, Miles.*

Clearing my throat, I manage to answer, "Um, a couple of years."

His dark eyes rake over me again, making me feel exposed despite the thin fabric clinging to my body. I shiver, even though it's warm in here. "Dom, sub, or switch?" he asks.

"Sub," I answer with a little more confidence this time. At least until he gives me a sexy smirk and I'm back to teetering on the edge of 'Holy fuck, he's so hot, I'm going to come' like I'm thirteen and not thirty.

Folding his arms over the top of the chair, he cocks his head. "How come we've never done a scene together? A couple of years is a long time not to cross paths. Especially in such a niche community."

That would be because I was too shy to approach you.

As tempting as it is to be honest and tell him exactly that, I just shrug. "You're in pretty high demand."

"Hmm." He pierces me with that intense stare again and I fight the urge to drop to my knees in supplication. "I can't help but think you'd also be popular at the club, too. A pretty boy like you is bound to get snapped up quickly."

My cock twitches under the compliment and it's all I can do not to whimper.

It's too much to hope that he won't notice, especially when I'm still standing and my crotch is basically at his eye level. Dmitri's lips quirk again. "So, you enjoy praise, then." It's not a question.

I nod anyway. "Yes, Sir." It's not my favorite title for a Dom, but it's more universal than the 'Daddy' that I prefer to use.

I guess I made a good choice, seeing as his eyes gleam. "Oh, *good boy.*"

This time I do whimper, and I reach for my dick, hoping to do *something* to calm it down. I can't get cum —or even precum— all over this costume before we start filming.

"*Tsk-tsk,*" Dmitri reaches out with one of his drool-worthy tattooed arms and gently curls his fingers around my wrist. "No touching, darling boy. Save it for the scene."

Ohhhhhh my god.

I find myself squirming and whining. "I...I...I..." My cheeks are on fire, the embarrassment of being so insanely hard under the bright lights of the studio, surrounded by people going about their daily jobs, is doing strange things to my nerve endings.

"Take a breath for me," Dmitri instructs, but his tone is patient and gentle. "Good. Now, what were you saying?"

"I'm" —I swallow roughly— "I'm *really* close to coming already."

It's humiliating to admit, especially to him. To my club crush. My experienced porn partner to be. But that just seems to make me more excited. I put that down to being a weird nerve thing.

"Can you tell me why that is?" he asks calmly and without judgment.

"Um," the part of me that thrives on praise wants to give in and be honest. But being honest means confessing my crush, and I don't think I can do that...although my stomach gets that pleasant twisty-coiling sensation at the renewed burst of embarrassment at the idea of it.

Dmitri arches an eyebrow and opens his mouth, then frowns. "I didn't get your name."

It's such a non-sequitur that I'm thrown out of my hazy, hyper-excited state almost instantly. "What?"

"Your name, sweetness. I didn't get it."

"Oh." I blink. In all the whirlwind of knowing who he was, I guess I didn't think it was important to introduce myself. "Um, it's Miles. *I'm* Miles."

"Miles," he repeats, as though he's testing the weight of my name on his tongue...and, *oh God*, why am I now thinking about his tongue? Thankfully, he distracts me by asking, "What's your screen name?"

"Oh. Uh," I start to blush and squirm again, "*Miles Deep*."

He snorts. "Well, it's better than Rod Steele. That's mine, by the way." I file that away as he tilts his head again and presses, "Is Miles your actual first name?"

"Yeah, it is. But, uh, the assistant who was helping me fill in my contract...they suggested Miles Deep. I can't take credit for it."

He chuckles and glances around the room. "That sounds like a Jamie idea."

"Is Jamie the assistant with the blue hair?" He nods and I grin. "Then, yeah. It was a Jamie idea."

After a beat, Dmitri asks, "Have you calmed down now, Miles?"

I can't put my finger on it, but there's something in the way he says my name so directly that has heat pooling in my belly again. Clearing my throat, I bob my head. "Y-yeah."

And there goes the eyebrow again. "Miles."

Fuck.

"I...I *am*. I just..."

He sits up straighter, arms still folded, the jacket straining against his biceps. That realization isn't helping my case as he waits in silence.

I sigh. "It's been a while for me," I finally admit, "and you..." I lick my lips, flames of embarrassment licking up the back of my neck and making the tips of my ears burn. "You're *you*."

"What does that mean?" I can't read his tone, but his stare is so sharp that I swear I feel it going straight through me.

"Th-the reason I've never approached you at the club..." *Am I really doing this?* My dick strains against the rough fabric holding it prisoner, seemingly loving my discomfort, the traitor. I swallow. "You're my club crush."

"Your" —he hesitates, and I want to die of mortification at the amusement I can see him trying to hide— "club crush."

There's no question there, but I nod anyway. "It's...it's silly, really, but I have this crush and, I don't know, I just..." I flap my hand wildly in the air in lieu of actually finishing the sentence.

"You were too shy to talk to me." Yeah, there's *definitely* amusement in his tone now. "Darling boy, that's adorable."

While the praise does all sorts of predictably wonderful things for my libido, the embarrassment from this whole exchange is also making me hot under the collar. That's either new, or I've never noticed how excited a little bit of shame can make me. Maybe because I'm usually balls deep in a scene with a Dom by the time any awkwardness hits.

"Well, you get me all to yourself today," he continues when I have no clue what to say. Then he snorts and gestures around the studio, "If you ignore the cameras and the crew, at least."

"It's not all that different to being at the club sometimes, is it?"

I think of the few times I've indulged in scenes with open doors, where other club members could watch or jerk off to whatever punishment my doms doled out. Come to think of it, those times had carried a similar thrill to the spikes of nervous arousal I felt when I was embarrassed. I guess I'd actually *liked* being on display.

"Not really, no. Especially if you think of Jake as another Dom, barking orders from his cushy director's chair."

I grin, glancing over to the diminutive man with the clipboard. "He did have Dom energy," I admit, making Dmitri laugh.

"Yeah, he does. But he's not actually our kind of kinky, as far as I know. Though he's done his research. It comes with the job, I guess."

I watch as Jake checks his watch and I realize I am probably about to be thrown in the deep end. "Speaking of the job," I hurry to try and prepare as best as possible, "do you...I mean, are there any things you want to do for this shoot? Things you want me to say or do?"

"I want you to enjoy yourself," he answers simply, then picks up the dossier at the table, flipping through the documents inside. I recognize my own handwriting. "Your hard limits are pretty much the same as mine," he adds after a beat, looking up at me seriously. "But I also don't like breath play, just so you're aware."

I nod, then gesture at his outfit, "It would be off-brand for Santa to choke someone —or be choked— anyway."

"Because it's not off-brand for Santa's beard to be brown and gray, or for him to be covered in tattoos?"

"Sexiest Santa Daddy ever," I mutter, before my own words catch up to me. My blush returns with a vengeance. "I mean—"

"*Oh*," he interrupts me, grinning widely now, "Santa *Daddy*, huh? Do you like that better than 'Sir' or 'Master'?"

"I don't mind either of those," I hedge, and regret it immediately when he gives me *the look* again.

"Miles."

"Yes," I admit after a long beat, squirming a little as I do. If we were already playing or in the middle of a scene, I'd expect to be punished for the hesitation. For not immediately correcting my behavior. "I like 'Daddy' better than those other titles. It feels...more personal, I guess."

"The Grove has a regression space. Are you a Little? Middle?"

I'm already shaking my head before he's even finished asking the question. "No, age regression isn't my thing. But...well, I do have a Daddy kink. I like Daddy doms. And you...I mean, you *look* like the perfect Daddy Dom, y'know? And by all accounts, you *act* like one. I mean, that's what I've heard from some of the other subs. But I won't call you Daddy if you aren't into that. I know it's not everyone's thing."

"As long as you're comfortable with it, I'd like it if you called me Daddy during our scenes," Dmitri smiles warmly up at me, not seeming at all perturbed by my nervous ramble. "I know a lot of subs and Littles believe the name has to be earned, and I respect that."

My heart gives a funny little squeeze and it's on the tip of my tongue to tell him that between my crush and his reputation, he's already earned the title...but that feels like it would be crossing some kind of line when we've only just met, so I shrug. "I'm comfortable with it." *It's actually a dream come true.* "Do you think Jake will mind?"

"Jake just needs us to last long enough to get him at least half an hour of decent footage."

"Half an hour?!" And now I'm back to being concerned about my stamina.

He chuckles. "We can come a couple of times in that window. Ideally, we'll perform for about forty-five minutes and then they'll edit it and polish it into a proper twenty-to-thirty minutes."

Not for the first time since I realized that I'd actually turned up to the wrong audition, I wonder what happened to the guy who should have been in my place. Would he have been better prepared to film forty-five minutes of sex with the hottest Santa ever? Probably.

But this has to be some kind of holiday season miracle, because that guy hasn't shown up, and I am about to experience something I have fantasized about for the past couple of years.

"I'll do my best," I say, cringing at how lame the words sound.

But Dmitri just gives me another one of those soft smiles, the skin at the edges of his eyes crinkling. "Good boy."

Chapter Four

I take it all back: taking on this project is the best life choice I've ever made. Is it still a cheesy Christmas-themed porn shoot? Yes. But it has introduced Miles into my life and, yeah, it has only been a handful of minutes so far, but I'm *excited* about getting to know him.

This kind of spark —this kind of connection— hasn't happened for me in longer than I'd like to admit. Things were getting stagnant. I was getting tired of it. Bored, even.

Then a hot-as-fuck sub stumbled into my porn scene, and it feels like a Christmas miracle. Especially because he wants to call me Daddy. At his own damn suggestion!

Maybe I crashed my car on my way here and this is all just a coma fantasy.

Honestly? If that's the case, leave my machines plugged in and don't bother trying to wake me up. I'm happy here.

I didn't know about my reputation at The Grove, though I should have guessed that the subs would compare notes about who they thought were the best doms to trust with their needs. It is flattering to hear that I was right up there with the best of them, and even more flattering to think that this muscular, gorgeous younger man was so taken by me that he was too shy to request a scene.

I just hope that I don't disappoint him today.

If I had my way, I would take him somewhere secluded and give him a show with all the bells and whistles. I'd make him writhe and pant and beg —at which point I would spank him for breaking my 'no begging' rule— and then give him the most dedicated aftercare he's ever had in his life.

I'm talking cleaning him up gently and carefully, getting him dressed into loose, soft clothes, snuggling with him and discussing the things he enjoyed about the scene, and the ways he might want to change it if we did it all again. I'm talking about making sure he's properly hydrated, or that he takes a nap if he needs one. Getting him food if he's snackish, or doing whatever his go-to comfort activities are with him. Being the best damn Daddy I can, basically.

Because while he might not be into regression, he was very specific about wanting not just a Dom, but a Daddy Dom. There's a certain extra expectation of nurturing that comes with the title, regardless of whether the sub in question sinks into a younger headspace or not. He wants a Daddy to take care of him just as badly as he wants to be dominated, and I love that he's open about that.

I love a man who knows what he wants.

I also love that what he wants aligns nicely with what I want, too.

Even if it is only for today's scene, though I try not to let that thought bring me down. Not when my gut is telling me that this could be the start of something special if only I let it happen at its own pace.

For all that Miles knows what he wants, he still seems a bit skittish. It could be the nerves about this being his first ever experience filming porn, but I think it's more than that. The surprise of recognizing me —and the cute awkwardness of confessing his 'club crush'— probably hasn't helped, either.

But then…he's paid to be here, and so am I. I'm sure his crush is legit, his body's reactions and his discomfort are too real to be anything other than that, but maybe he's concerned that I'm only playing with him because that's what I signed up for.

"Don't be nervous," I tell him, smiling warmly. "You look perfect, and the camera is going to love you. You've got this, and I'm here if you need to safe word out, okay?"

He does seem to settle a bit, a sweet blush rising to his cheeks. "Thanks. I'm, uh, I'm looking forward to doing this scene with you."

My stomach swoops a little at how earnest he sounds and I open my mouth to flirt in return, but then Jake calls for our attention.

Break time is apparently over, and now it's showtime.

***

After running through the general process for Miles's benefit, reassuring our newbie that we do take breaks to clean up, hydrate, and let our bodies recover for the next round, Jake gives us some idea of the positions he wants to see us in, and the overall tone for the scene. He looks over at me with a wry smirk. "That last shoot we did together was a hit, but people asked for more 'connection' after that one. So maybe try to go softer and slower. I mean, it *is* Christmas, guys. Let's make some sweet and sexy holiday love for the people, hmm? Apparently romance isn't dead. Who knew?"

It's a rhetorical question and we all take our places at his barked command. I blow a kiss to Ricky, one of the two camera guys, as I saunter past to stand behind the fake door. He's straight, as far as I'm aware, but always captures the most flattering angles with his footage. He raises his middle finger towards me right before Jake settles back into his chair and yells "Action!"

Nobody's had the heart to tell Jake that this isn't Hollywood. He pays so well that it feels cruel to take that from him.

After fixing my silly red hat and grabbing the matching big, red bag of fake presents, I knock on the door and wait only a few seconds before it swings inwards. Leaning casually inside the false doorframe, I give Miles a moment to exaggeratedly look me over from head-to-toe and then back again.

"*Santa*," he breathes with what sounds like giddy delight. He widens his eyes and bats his lashes. "What a big sack you have! What's in there for me?"

With the rolling of the cameras, I can't give in to the bark of startled laughter that threatens to burst from my chest. He was all cute and awkward only a few minutes ago, but now...now he's confident and, if I'm not mistaken, a little bratty.

There's *definitely* a glint of challenge in his pretty blue eyes.

"Actually, Miles," I drop the bag carelessly to the ground, but his gaze stays planted on mine, "you're on the naughty list this year."

He gasps, grabbing the lapels of my jacket to tug me forward. The door swings shut behind me just before he shoves me back against it, thankfully not so hard as to rattle the whole set.

"*Oh no*, Santa," he affects a sultry pleading tone, running his fingertips over my chest teasingly, "I'm not a naughty boy." He starts to sink to his knees on the faux-hardwood floor, beseeching, "Can I show you how *nice* I can be?"

It feels very much like the rug has been pulled out from underneath me. I went into this expecting to have to lead the scene, to coach him through nerves about performing on camera, but Miles has taken me completely by surprise here.

My cock *loves* his confidence, even while I ache to discipline the playful brattiness and challenge right out of him.

Carding my fingers into his dark hair, I marvel briefly at its softness. The generic 'more on top' style suits him, but it doesn't look like it would feel as silky as it does, slipping between my digits.

I yank his head back just enough to tilt his chin upwards, and I grin at the flash of need in his expression.

He's so responsive...

"You have to work really hard if you want me to call you a good boy, Miles." I tell him.

Bless him, he takes the obvious pun and runs with it, "I like it when things are *really hard*, Santa."

"I'll bet you do."

The cheeky fucker winks at me.

Oh, it is on!

My fingers curl in his hair, tightening their grip, tugging just enough to make those pretty blue eyes widen with more genuine surprise and a hint of pain.

Good.

"Undo my belt," I demand.

"Yes, D—*Santa.*"

I feel myself twitch at the slip of his tongue, and I am already so fucking done being 'Santa', it isn't even funny. I want to hear the right word falling from those plump, pink lips of his. "What did you almost call me?"

His throat works convulsively, his Adam's apple bobbing. "I…"

"Miles." Fuck, but I love the way his pupils dilate when I say his name in that authoritative tone. He loves it, I can tell. A quick glance down at the darkening patch of red towel-like fabric over his crotch confirms it. I double down. "Say it. Say what you really want to call me."

"Oh fuck," he murmurs, his cheeks flushing pink.

Finally, the dynamic feels the way I expected it to, but now I know to watch out for his sass. He's going to keep me on my toes today; I can feel it.

"Say it." I pull just a touch harder on his hair and he moans.

"*Daddy*," the title comes out on a needy rush of air. "B-because you're *Father* Christmas…and you look like a Daddy."

My dick goes from already interested to straining for attention instantly. It's all I can do to bite back the praise he would enjoy so much. We can't rush this. Namely because it would be the most disappointing porn flick ever if we did, but also because I don't *want* to rush this. I want to draw it out. To see just how much teasing Miles can take.

"That's what I thought," I say, then jerk my chin downwards. "Didn't I tell you to undo my belt?"

"Yes, Daddy." His fingers scramble for the buckle, working as quickly as he can to obey the command. Once it's undone, he sits back on his heels and waits for further instruction.

Perfect.

"Take it off and get my dick out."

The flush to his cheeks seems to brighten, but his movements are sure and steady as he slips the belt free of the pant loops and then drops it to the floor. His eyes meet mine and stay there as he unbuttons the pants and draws down the zipper.

I swear my cock actually springs free with a bouncy sound effect the moment it gets a run at freedom, but my gaze is locked on his.

When he doesn't immediately reach for my erection, I nod with satisfaction. "Good."

Miles whines, clearly expecting the other half of the statement.

"Open your mouth," I tell him, inching my hips forward when he greedily complies, "but do not suck."

There's disbelief in those beautiful baby blues now, and that only makes me harder.

I groan as I slide between those parted lips, though. Miles's mouth feels every bit as perfect as it looks. He keeps his jaw lax while I slowly rock my length in and out of the warm, wet space he's offering, but I can see how badly he wants to close his lips around me.

"Uh-uh," I waggle my index finger at him when he presses the heel of his palm down against his own crotch. "Boys who want to get on Santa's nice list need to wait for permission to touch themselves."

He whines again, this time squirming a bit.

"No, Miles."

He goes rigid, cheeks impossibly pink. There's a hint of panic in his eyes, along with embarrassment. During our debrief with Jake, I reminded Miles that standard safe word rules still apply, and if he needs to tap out all he has to do is say 'red' or 'red light'. He's experienced enough with club play that I trust he will do exactly that if he needs to.

Still, this is our first time together, and I wouldn't be a good Daddy —or Dom, for that matter— if I didn't check in.

"You okay? You've got permission to speak right now."

He pulls back from my cock and nods. "I'm good, Daddy. Just..." Glancing away, he startles only a little when he seems to recall exactly where we are, but I don't think the jolt in the set of his shoulders would be noticeable to anyone other than me. Swallowing roughly, he looks back up, "I...almost came."

I'd thought he was exaggerating earlier about being on a hair-trigger, but the surge of pride and desire I feel at being responsible for taking him to the edge so quickly is something else. My dick twitches, a dribble of the proof of how arousing Miles's admission is taking us both a little by surprise.

I watch as his gaze tracks the fluid as it slips from my head and down my shaft.

"Lick that up," I demand, then moan as he does.

It takes a ridiculous amount of effort to remind myself that I have a job to do here. That we're roleplaying for the cameras.

Clearing my throat, my voice comes out gruff when I say, "You have to tell me when you get too close, Miles. Daddy doesn't want you to make a mess in your jammies. Not on Christmas Eve."

There, back on track. Kind of.

"I need to get back on your nice list," he nods, once again pulling back from my dick, this time with even more reluctance than before. Then his lips curl and the defiance from earlier is back. "Unless you prefer naughty boys, Daddy?"

Oh. My. Fucking. God.

Chapter Five

Years of theater training. That's what I put my burst of confidence down to. Theater training and my time spent at The Grove. What else could explain how perfectly easy it is to perform like this for these people and the cameras?

Dmitri's dick, maybe?

It is a thing of beauty all on its own, it's true. I mean, is he bigger than most of the men I've been with? No. Thicker? Also no. But there's something about the perfect curve of it, the way it arches up to meet his soft belly, glaringly clean skinned while surrounded by so much inked flesh.

But...no. That beautiful cock is not the reason I'm so comfortable doing this.

Dmitri himself?

Yeah...that might be hitting closer to the mark. He's big and tattooed and intimidating at first glance, but beneath that façade there's a gentleness that settles me. Even when he was yanking my head backwards, it was controlled and done with care. The pain he inflicted was just enough to ride that line between 'ouch' and 'I'm about to come'. Literally.

I can't believe how close I just got from a tiny bit of hair pulling and some firm words from a Daddy Dom.

Not just any Daddy Dom, though. My *dream* Daddy Dom.

So far, he's been everything he's reputed to be and then some.

In all of my daydreams, I've imagined being his good boy. I've pictured myself submitting flawlessly, earning praises that not only warm my soul, but bring me to new heights of desire and need.

But now that I've got him in front of me, I'm bratting.

Me. Goody-two-shoes Miles Jeffries. Bratting.

For *Dmitri*. For the man I want to hear nothing but praise from.

What the fuck is going on with me?

I want him to enjoy this. Selfishly, I want him to enjoy it so damn much that maybe we might do it again at the club, or at my place, or at his. Without the cheesy costumes. Without the cameras. Without the fucking director. Just us. Just Daddy and Boy. Alone.

So why am I pushing boundaries? Why am I testing him?

It's gotta be the cameras.

I am 'yes, and'ing my way through a porn scene.

This is *not* the big break I'm going to write home to Mom about.

But, if I stop and think about it, there's something extra exciting about doing this. While I've never thought badly of anyone who works in the adult film industry, it's never been something I would have said I wanted to do. But now that I'm here...

Yeah.

This is *hot*.

Not just Dmitri, even though he is extremely hot.

But just being on a porn set. Having fully-dressed people watching me —watching *us*— as things get hot and heavy.

Knowing that those same people are going to see so much more. Knowing that *other people* are going to watch this on their phones or laptops or, hell, even their TVs. They're going to see me wearing this silly onesie, whimpering and admitting to almost coming in my pants within *seconds* of being ordered around and...*oh, God.*

My balls are tight again, that tell-tale tingle making me squirm on the spot.

Do I...do I have a humiliation kink?

I was all revved up earlier when I was embarrassed in front of Dmitri, but I put that down to it being *Dmitri*. But now...

Fuck.

The thought of embarrassing myself in front of the people in this studio, or the hundreds —maybe *thousands*— of people who pay to watch the finished video...

Shit. Shit, shit, shit.

I need to stop thinking about it, or I am actually going to blow my load, and I haven't even blown Santa yet!

Okay, so that is going to the top of the list of sentences I never thought I'd say. Or think.

"Santa doesn't reward naughty boys," Dmitri practically growls the words at me, and it takes me a long moment to remember that I just playfully offered to be naughty.

My cock throbs, and I don't know if that's in warning or desperation at this point.

Still, instead of behaving —of bowing my head and being a good, pliant little sub— I jut my chin higher. "I made it onto that list for a reason...and you wouldn't be here if you didn't like that, would you, Santa?"

Surprise, arousal, and then determination flit across his handsome features before he grabs my bicep and shoves me towards the large bed in the middle of the room. I'm vaguely aware of his boots and pants being toed off and left behind with his belt as he crosses the space in two long-legged strides.

He sits on the edge of the mattress facing our audience, those bare, tattooed legs spread wide, his delicious dick jutting up proudly, and then he pats his thigh. "Over my lap, Miles."

Oh fuck.

"You've earned a spanking for your sass," he adds. "Fifteen. You'll count as I go."

When I bring a trembling hand to the zipper of my long johns, he shakes his head.

"Stay dressed."

I'm aware of the damp patch of precum spreading across my crotch where my cock has leaked so much, I'm almost afraid that I did come without realizing it. The embarrassment from that, combined with the knowledge that this spanking will most definitely push me over the edge, has me biting my lip.

"You're not allowed to come, either," Dmitri adds the caveat right as I'm bending over his lap, and I jolt, unable to prevent the distressed whine from escaping.

"You've already made enough of a mess of your Christmas jammies, haven't you?"

My cheeks burn and my cock weeps some more while I nod, "Yes, Daddy."

"If you *do* come," he warns, "you don't get to suck my cock."

"*Nooo*," the protest slips out before I can stop it, and he chuckles, smoothing a big, beefy hand down my spine. Then his fingers pause at the top of my ass, fiddling with something and—*Oh.*

Suddenly, the warmth of my onesie is gone, replaced by cool air over my ass. He's undone the two buttons holding the cute butt-flap in place, and now I'm exposed.

My ass is on camera for all the world to see.

Another jolt of that weird excitement tinged with humiliation barrels through me.

I'm going to be immortalized on film being spanked to orgasm by the hottest Santa alive.

I squeeze my eyes shut and breathe deeply.

That last thought was almost too much. The dampness at my crotch feels uncomfortably wet now, smushed between my body and Dmitri's thigh.

I jerk forward uncontrollably as Dmitri's hand gently cups my ass cheek. "What's your safe word?"

"Red, Daddy," I answer.

"Hmm. Maybe we should make it 'Rudolph'," he muses, warming the skin he's found with broad circles of his palm, "seeing as your ass is about to glow red like his nose."

It's difficult not to laugh, but the really lame joke does the job of distracting me from almost coming. I wonder if that was his goal. Either way, I'm glad for it.

"Rudolph it is," I agree, still with a hint of sass.

Why can't I stop talking?

He snorts. "Remember, Miles, you're counting out loud." Then, before I can properly brace for it, his hand comes down on me with a resounding '*smack*'. It stings and my eyes water.

"Fu—*uh*—one."

Yeah, that was convincing.

He's going to think I'm the worst sub ever.

SMACK!

I jolt forward with a yelp. "Two."

Three, four, and five follow rapidly.

Then a few more.

My cock is really paying attention around number nine.

Dmitri's blows aren't as hard now, but they sting when they meet the flesh he has heated up. My ass cheeks feel like they're on fire, throbbing in time with my heartbeat.

I love every second of it.

When number ten lands, I moan the number and rut into his thigh.

"No coming, precious," he reminds me, and my brain almost short-circuits.

Precious?

It's not quite 'good boy', but it's praiseful enough that I whimper and writhe, my belly swooping with ecstasy.

Fuuuuuuck.

"E-eleven, t-t-twelve," I stammer over the next two slaps to my behind, trying to focus on the pain rather than the coil of tension tightening inside me. I'm getting close. I'm going to break his rule. I'm going to humiliate myself on camera, in front of countless people.

And I love that, too.

I love that idea so much that—

"Th—*ohhhh*—thirt—t-teen."

Oh.

Oh no.

"Daddy! *Daddy*..." I tried to hold it back. I really, really did. But that last smack has sent me careening right over the edge, my hips convulsing with the sheer force of my orgasm. It feels like I come forever, my dick twitching and jerking where it's still smushed against Dmitri's thigh and...*fuck*. I've just come all over his leg. Yes, I'm wearing clothes, but the fabric is thin, and it was already wet...

My cheeks —all of them— burn hot, the ones on my face in shame.

But, *Jeeeesus,* does that shame feel good.

How have I never noticed this about myself before?

Because you've always been a good boy, I realize as I catch my breath, still grinding forward into Dmitri's leg, trying to wring out every last moment of pleasure. *I've never really done anything to make myself feel so humiliated.*

Dmitri's dark chuckle brings me back to myself. "You're definitely on my naughty list now," he says. "Two more to go, baby."

I cry out when fourteen lands, my skin so much more sensitive after a brief reprieve and an epic orgasm.

"Count it," he insists.

"Fourteen," I gasp out, then jolt and add, "Fifteen!" with emphatic relief, slumping over his lap, hypersensitive and exhausted.

Dmitri's big hand settles between my shoulder blades, and he strokes down my back gently. Then he bends over me and murmurs, "Good boy."

And I...burst into tears.

Chapter Six

"**C**ut!" Jake calls out while I'm in the process of manhandling Miles into my lap for a cuddle. I tune Jake and the rest of the small crew out, knowing that everyone on board is well-versed in BDSM and, in particular, my feelings on providing proper aftercare. They'll give us space and wait for my signal to proceed when I'm good and ready.

Miles goes practically boneless in my arms, tucking his face into the crook of my neck as he sniffles and hiccups, easing out of what I can only assume is sub drop. Stroking his back, I kiss his sweaty temple and nuzzle my beard into the side of his face, murmuring, "I've got you, precious. You did so good for me. I'm here for whatever you need, okay?"

That first scene was surprisingly intense. I went into it expecting a blow job, maybe some frotting, and a lot of silly Christmas-themed puns, and I would have enjoyed that.

But what I got was an introduction to Miles as a sub.

And wow.

Wow.

He's a bit of a contradiction. He clearly craves —and obviously gets off on— praise, but he's determined to push boundaries and make getting that praise even harder for himself. He seems to want to be good, but *needs* to be a brat. He's bashful and shy…and then *really* enjoys performing for people. I even think he might have a bit of a humiliation kink, which he didn't mention earlier but which would have been good to know because I probably wouldn't have gone straight into spanking, considering how close to the edge I'd known he was.

Still, watching him fall apart was glorious.

The way his lips had parted and his eyes fluttered shut, long, dark lashes dusting rosy, red cheeks. The way he'd whined 'Daddy'; panicked, apologetic, but with a touch of euphoria…Fuck, I've never been so close to coming untouched during a scene, either.

"I'm sorry," he whispers, barely loud enough for me to catch, completely pulling me out of my happy musings.

I frown and rest my cheek against him, tempted to try and get him to make eye-contact, but not wanting to make his comedown uncomfortable. "Why?"

"I broke the rule," his breath turns shuddery, before his tone takes on a steely, self-deprecating edge, "*and* I started crying. Jesus. That's *so* hot in porn, isn't it?"

"Dacryphilia is actually a kink…" I muse, then snort when he pulls back to give me a flat, unimpressed stare. The expression turns startled when I smile and kiss the tip of his nose. "But the crying is just the come down from the rush of endorphins and stuff." A stray thought hits me. "Is that the first time you've cried from sub drop?"

"I…" Miles pauses, tilting his head to the side. "That quickly and unexpectedly? Yeah. I mean, I've been irritable after scenes, maybe a bit weepy and depressive a couple of hours later, but…nothing that sudden."

Still stroking his back, I keep my tone gentle as I prod, "What made this time different, do you think?"

"Aside from the fact that it was with you, and I guess I put you on a pedestal —a totally valid one, so far, by the way— I guess...well, there was a lot going on."

"Can you talk me through that?"

"I, uh," he clears his throat and looks away, "I just discovered that I have a bit of a humiliation kink, I think. And, um, that I *really* like the idea of people watching me. Us. That's never really been a thing for me before, but...well, I haven't done many performative scenes, either. They're usually one-on-one. Maybe with only one other couple watching. But this..." Miles sits up a bit straighter and waves his hand around the studio. "This is an actual *audience*, y'know? Not other kinky people who are also naked and vulnerable, but...people who are fully dressed and seemingly impassive and...*holy shit*, yeah, that's...that's a surprising new turn-on for me." He glances down the length of his body, where the outline of his spent dick is already firming up again, more than obvious through the wet mess he's made of himself. His blush comes back. "*Wow.*"

Fuck me, but he's adorable.

"So, you had no idea you enjoy being embarrassed? Or that you've got an exhibitionist kink?" He shakes his head and at least that explains why he didn't say anything earlier.

I smile. "Well, they do go hand-in-hand nicely."

"Yeah," he looks down again, rueful, and scrunches his nose. "I would have said something. I mean, you knew about the praise kink, and you dragged that out, so..."

"We've got plenty of time to play around with all your kinks, precious, don't worry. But, for now," I gesture towards his crotch, "let me clean you up, okay?"

"Okay, Daddy."

The way my heart skips a beat over the sweetly spoken agreement, with Miles still a little soft and pliant from the scene and the orgasm, spikes a tiny frisson of terror inside me.

This is just part of our roles, I tell myself, even though I know the cameras aren't rolling and Miles is at his most open, genuine and vulnerable. *Do not get attached.*

I'm a little concerned that it's already too late for that.

Some professional I am.

***

"Are you comfortable continuing?" I ask Miles once he's clean and has changed into a pair of bright red boxer briefs which have molded to his skin and leave nothing to the imagination.

I'm wearing my long, red jacket like a robe, cinched around my belly with a long length of fuzzy white material which I think has actually been borrowed from a bathrobe. My legs are bare, and I keep catching Miles's gaze lingering on the tops of my hairy thighs.

We've hydrated, and I made sure he snacked on some celery and carrot sticks, as well as a handful of grapes to replenish his energy. He nods and I signal to Jake that we're good to go.

He sets the thermos of coffee he was drinking from down on the snacks cart and heads back over to his seat.

"That first scene was capital H *hot*, guys," he declares enthusiastically. "Your chemistry is off the charts."

"No notes?" Miles asks, and I arch an eyebrow at him, confused by the question, until he follows with, "You told us to make love and then we, uh...went a bit off-script, so to speak."

Jake just grins wider and shakes his head, mousy brown hair flopping into his eyes before he brushes it back. "Nah; that was *much* better than some vanilla lovey-dovey stuff. You're a natural, kid. Keep playing it up for the cameras. People are gonna eat this up."

"And there's nothing specific you want us to do in this next scene?" Miles prods a little more. "Just...pick up from where we left off, or...?"

"Actually," using his fingertips, Jake taps his lips thoughtfully, "why don't we imply a little time jump, hmm? Maybe Miles feels the need to feed Santa some cookies and milk to make up for being such a naughty boy. *That* is sweet, right?"

Miles's eyes light up. "Oh, I like that idea."

That doesn't surprise me.

Jake claps his hands together. "Perfect. Let's move the bed out of the way and set you guys up on the rug in front of the fireplace and tree."

And that's how I find myself reclining against the feet of a comfortable-looking armchair, wearing only my jacket draped over my shoulders as a scantily dressed Boy handfeeds me cookies.

Crumbs tumble down and get stuck in my beard and in the coarse hair over my chest, but Miles tells me not to worry about them.

He's kneeling between my spread thighs, smiling coyly. "I'll clean them up for you, Santa Daddy."

"And how will you—*oh*." His mouth is on my skin, sucking kisses over the soft mound of my belly and up my pecs, his wet tongue darting out to lick the crumbs away as he travels up my body.

I can't wait to see how this is going to look on film. Him, with his smooth, unblemished, muscular body pressed up against my softer, rounded, hairy and heavily tattooed one. His arguably much more youthful features next to mine, cleanshaven and sweet against my bearded gruffness.

He gently nibbles the crumbs from my beard and peppers kisses along my jawline before he reaches my lips.

"That *was* very nice," I murmur softly into the charged air between us, my eyes locked on his. "What else do nice boys do?"

That tempting pink tongue darts out, wetting his lips and getting rid of any remaining traces of the cookies. He swallows roughly, then practically whispers, "They kiss their Daddies."

"Are you a nice boy, Miles?"

He nods.

"Then what are you waiting for?" I goad him playfully, then gasp when he slots his mouth over mine, leading us in a slow, sensual kiss.

In this moment, I definitely forget that we're acting. That we're being paid to do any of this. That he's not really my Boy, and I'm not really his Daddy. It's impossible to believe that this is all just a scene.

Because this kiss...

This kiss is *electric*.

Miles has stolen my breath and —as dramatic as it sounds— my heart in one swift, sweet move, and he's got no fucking idea that it has happened. One second, I'm performing a semi-planned-out porn scene, the next, my heart is beating rapidly, and I can't gather my thoughts.

All from a kiss.

I've had countless kisses over the years. On screen, in the clubs, and with romantic partners...but none of them have felt so instantly overwhelming. I've never felt quite so topsy-turvy after just a kiss, either. And I've certainly never said something as asinine as someone stealing my heart from one before.

I have no way to explain why this one feels so different, though. It just does.

Maybe it's the mistletoe.

My inner voice thinks he's hilarious.

The mistletoe in question is fake and is currently suspended above us on fishing wire.

Also, everyone knows mistletoe magic only works in December...and we're only *faking* that it's Christmas right now.

But still, there's nothing fake about the way Miles's tongue is teasing mine, slowly twisting and twirling around it like it's doing some kind of sensual dance. There's nothing fake about the way he's melted into me, all breathy sighs and mewls of delight. There's nothing fake about his fingers clutching at my shoulder blades, or the softness of his hair between my own fingers as I cup the back of his head.

"Daddy," he whines against my lips when we part for necessary oxygen, "Santa...I need..." His hips rock forward, the cotton of his briefs doing nothing to restrain the hard bulge that bumps against my own aching dick.

"You need Daddy's cock, don't you, Miles?"

"Please," he breathes, and I force myself to pull back to look at him, only to find his eyes shut, his cheeks rosy again. "Please," he repeats.

"It is *very* nice of you to ask so politely."

His eyes flutter open and he bites his lip while his hand skirts down the length of my body to fondle my erection. "Santa...Daddy...*Please.*"

It's almost like that first orgasm earlier knocked the brat right out of him. Or maybe it was the spanking. Either way, *this* Miles is yielding and sweet, and I have the sudden urge to give him everything his heart desires.

He's like the human embodiment of that Puss in Boots gif with the big round eyes you just can't say no to.

He's dangerous in all the best ways.

"You're not getting your mouth on it, precious," I remind him, smirking when he makes an exaggerated sound of disappointment. "I warned you what would happen if you came in your jammies earlier."

Instead of arguing with me or sassing with me, he nods. "I know. But it's such a gorgeous cock, Santa."

"One might even say it's jolly right now. If we put a Santa hat on it, we could call it Jolly Old Saint Dick."

The expression on Miles's face is hilarious, but he quickly schools it back into something a bit more reminiscent of his earlier bratting. Eyes gleaming, and neatly sidestepping my admittedly clumsy pun, he says, "I have to be careful with it, though."

I'm going to regret this; I just know it.

"Why?" I ask.

"Because Santa only comes once a year," he answers, lips curling all the way up with his ridiculous joke. "And if that's really the case, I want to make it an epic orgasm."

It's all I can do not to groan. I guess I deserved that for reaching with the 'jolly' thing.

Cupping his jaw, I rub my thumb over his cheekbone and, bringing our lips to a point of nearly touching, I wait until he begins to part his before I murmur, "Get on the bed, Miles."

"*Argh.*" His quiet sound of frustration is music to my ears. I swat his perfectly rounded ass in warning, gentle with my touch, knowing that he's still probably a bit sensitive after the spanking.

"And take those off," I add, gesturing at his underwear. "You're not going to need them for this."

Chapter Seven

I 'm naked in front of the cameras. In front of the film crew. In front of Dmitri.

I'm naked, and I'm on all fours.

I'm naked, and I'm on all fours, and I'm *loving* it.

I'm loving being on display. I'm loving my lack of control over what happens next. I'm loving the fact that Dmitri is about to fuck me.

At least, I hope he's about to fuck me.

My punishment for earlier was that I'm not allowed to suck him off, which does feel like a tragedy all on its own. But I'm still going to enjoy his dick in other ways. I mean, it would be a disappointing porn video if I didn't, wouldn't it?

"Look at you," Dmitri purrs from behind me. "All ready for my North Pole, aren't you?"

Oh my god, the puns are going to kill me if the wait for his dick doesn't.

But I'm being a good sub right now, so I bob my head. "*Please,* Daddy."

"Patience, precious."

I open my mouth to protest —or beg again— but all that comes out is a gasp as his warm, wet tongue laps over my hole. He does it again and again, using his big, tattooed hands to part my cheeks and really go to town, tickling my skin with his beard.

I lose track of what I'm saying, of my pleas and curses and babbled obscenities. All I can feel is his mouth and that tongue, slowly spearing its way inside me, filling me and prepping me for a thorough stuffing, like the luckiest of stockings.

Oh, god, now I'm thinking puns I'm not even going to get a chance to use.

When a thick finger joins in with his tongue, stretching me out so he can lick and —*holy fuck*— suck even deeper, I throw my weight onto my left forearm so I can reach underneath myself and...

"Uh-uh," Dmitri chides, biting at my still-tender ass cheek. "No playing with yourself. That pleasure is all mine."

I know better than to complain about this new rule, but I can't help whining. "Daddy, I need..."

"You'll get my candy cane, precious. Just be patient."

Oh, sure, I can be patient. I'm just going to combust first.

"You —*ah!* — you only get to call it a candy cane if I can suck on it."

My impatience is making me bratty and I brace myself for the punishment, trying not to whine as the magical tongue and finger disappear from the place I want them most.

"Miles..." Dmitri's voice is calm and even mildly amused. I feel his palms running over my ass again. It's a warning. "Whose fault was it that you're *not* getting to suck on Santa's candy cane, hmm?"

"M-mine," I answer, trying to sound remorseful and not like I'm desperate to just get back what we were doing. "My fault, Santa. Daddy. I know."

He chuckles and rubs over the flesh that is still a bit raw and tingly from earlier. I try not to think about our audience this time, but I'm getting a bit twitchy knowing that the cameras are probably aimed right at my pink cheeks. "And what do you think happens to naughty boys who complain about the punishments they've rightfully earned?"

Swallowing, I offer, "More punishments? A...another spanking?"

"Well, I still want to fuck this pretty ass of yours, darling boy, so no. No spanking." I don't know if I'm relieved or disappointed to hear that, but he continues, effectively distracting me, "No...I think maybe we need to cover up that mouth of yours so you can't get yourself in more trouble."

He climbs off the bed and I turn my body a little to watch as he picks up the red bag he'd entered the scene with. His cock bobs with his movement, but he pays it no mind, too busy with his prop.

Santa's got a full sack, I think yet another ridiculous pun, barely managing to conceal my snort while he goes digging inside it.

"Lucky for you, the elves have sent lots of presents to help at a time like this," he says, then pulls out a ball gag. "What's your traffic light color, Miles?"

Oh, god, people are going to see me in a gag while a man wearing half a Santa suit fucks me.

"Green," I practically moan. "Like...*neon* green. With sparkles."

Dmitri arches an eyebrow, his lips twitching underneath his luscious beard. "Good boy."

My cock jerks, dribbling the evidence of how much I liked that. As desperately as I want to, I do not reach for it.

The mattress dips as he straddles my hips and leans over my body, his soft, furry belly rubbing along the dip in my spine. I arch up instinctively, and he brings the gag to my mouth, holding the two ends of the leather strap on either side of my face. "Open wide, precious."

I do as I'm told, closing my mouth as best I can around the solid, round intrusion. With the drape of Daddy's open jacket, I feel completely cloaked in him, and I love it. Then he sits back a bit, securing the gag around the back of my head, and I lament the fact that we can't kiss anymore.

I wonder if he feels as punished by this discovery as I do.

The bratty, belligerent part of me which has come out to play today hopes that he does.

Dmitri hands me a tinkling Christmas bell. "If you need to safe word," he tells me, "give it a shake. Understood?"

I nod. He instructs me to demonstrate and I do.

"Now," he settles behind me again, and the hair of his legs brushes my bare thighs while his sticky cockhead bumps over the curve of my ass where it meets the base of my spine, "if you're a good boy and you do not come, I will take the gag out when I'm done. Nod if you understand. Ring the bell if you have questions or don't consent."

I nod enthusiastically.

I can hear the smile in his voice when he says, "Good. You're going to let me finish what I was doing earlier, aren't you?"

"Mmmhmmm," I manage around the gag, nodding again.

Then the warmth of his skin on mine retreats, and his hands part my cheeks again, and I cry out when he dives back in without warning or gentle preamble. My fingers scrabble at the sheets, and I whine and rock back onto his tongue and what is now two of his fingers, fucking myself with wild abandon. My mouth is stretched wide around the gag and between that and my heavy, panted breaths, I am drooling over my chin and down onto the sheets.

I must look wrecked.

I definitely feel wrecked.

"Mmm," Dmitri's teeth graze my left ass cheek, and he soothes the sting with a sweet kiss, still pistoning his fingers in and out of me, "you're doing so well so far, precious." He crooks his fingers, probing and prodding until—

"*Mmmrrraaaaa!*" I can't contain the strangled sound, not even around the gag.

"Looks like I found your magic spot. Isn't that right, darling boy?"

I will not come. I will not come.

Dmitri twists his fingers and prods at my prostate again. I whimper, pushing back hard.

"You're so responsive, Miles. Such a good boy for Daddy. Maybe you'll make it onto my nice list after all."

With the gag in my mouth, the babbled nonsense I want to spill comes out as a mumbled mess of "Mmmhmmm mmmhhhmmmhhmmhmmm."

It's honestly a miracle that I don't shoot a load all over the bedsheets at this point. Especially with his praise making my belly flip and my heart race.

"That's it, honey, ride my fingers. Show me how much you want my cock."

I do exactly that, completely shamelessly, begging and pleading around the gag, the sounds giving away my meaning even while the words are mangled. I increase my volume when he takes the fingers away, only settling when I hear the click of a bottle snapping open.

Oh my god. Yes. Yes, please. Yes.

Three fingers press inside me soon after, slippery and a bit cool from the lube, but I sink back onto them, welcoming the stretch and the burn.

"Fuck, you're taking that so well, darling boy."

"*Nnnnggghhh.*" I'm close to having to use the bell. Not because I'm uncomfortable, but because I'm afraid I will go over the edge again.

Breaking that rule once during the shoot, I'm fine with.

If I do it a second time, I don't think I can ever look myself in the mirror again. If I come, it would push me into a level of shame and embarrassment that isn't kinky or enjoyable. It would make me feel like I'm a bad sub, not being able to follow a simple instruction.

Do. Not. Come. I think, bending forward to glare in the direction of my disobedient dick. *Don't you even fucking think about—*

"*Nnngnmmgbbbnnn.*"

My whole body tenses up, with Dmitri having stroked my prostate again.

One more tiny bump to that sensitive bundle of nerves and I'll be a goner.

"You've been such a good boy, Miles," Dmitri coos the commendation as he slowly withdraws his fingers, and I'm so distracted by relief that the praise, thankfully, does little more than give me a bit of a buzz. "So I'm going to remove the gag and you're going to roll onto your back, legs spread, ready for my cock."

Thank you, Santa. Thank you, the three ghosts of Christmas. Thank you, Dasher and Prancer and...Tequila and Moscato, or whatever the other reindeer are called.

Thank you, thank you, thank you.

We shuffle around and I sit in the middle of the bed, holding still as he gently undoes the leather straps. He tosses the used toy aside, and it lands on the floor with a solid thump, which we both ignore. I work my jaw to ease the ache. Dmitri reaches out with those big, strong hands of his and cups either side of my face, massaging gently.

"You did so good, Miles," he reiterates, this time softly and with a warmth that makes my throat feel tight.

He's not expecting any sort of reply from me, though, instead dipping his head down to kiss me. It's a surprisingly sweet kiss, for how insanely erotic this whole scene has been so far. Just a brush of his lips to mine, without any pushing for more, though I part my lips for him anyway.

I'm so weak for him, it's not even funny.

I sigh as his tongue slips into my mouth, teasing mine — caressing it, even.

I whimper and chase after him when he lazily draws away, hitching my thighs up his sides while his cockhead nudges at my entrance, blood-hot and thick.

"You still want my dick, precious?"

"Yes. Fuck yes. Green light, Daddy."

That's all he needs before he pushes inside, driving in steadily, but slowly, making sure that I feel every glorious inch. We both groan and pant, and when he's fully seated, his balls nestled snugly above the curve of my cheeks, he leans down to kiss me again.

This time the kiss is sloppier. Needier. Filthier. It's all tongue and wetness and barely restrained desperation.

Then he starts to talk, murmuring delicious, dirty praises as his hips begin a torturously slow roll and grind.

"You feel so good, Miles. So tight around me. Fuck, you fit me like a glove."

"Daddy," I gasp as his rolling nudges that spot inside me that makes me see stars, "Daddy, please. I need…"

"What do you need? Say it, Miles." He thrusts again with a bit more force, aiming for that same spot and hitting his mark with unfair accuracy. I arch from the mattress, crying out, but he insists, "Say it."

"More!" I cry, the word bursting from somewhere deep in my chest. "More, Daddy! H-harder —*ohhh*— faster. Fuck me hard. *Use me.*"

"Oh, *God,*" his curse is guttural and raw, sending tingles from my toes to my brain and back again, "you're such. A. Good. Boy." Every word is punctuated with a hard thrust, gradually increasing in force and speed. I'm starting to see stars. Little bolts of lightning igniting in my veins.

"Daddy," it's less word and more like ninety percent air as it's pushed from me with every delightfully rough shove of his hips and slap of skin connecting, "Daddy. Daddy. *Ah. Daddy.*"

Pressure has well and truly built at the base of my spine, and it's all I can do to try and ignore the feeling of Dmitri's belly rubbing along my cock with each movement. My balls have drawn up so tightly, I'm convinced they'll be permanently stuck this way. I'm tingling all over, my heart racing and brain completely mush.

"Oh, *precious,*" Dmitri groans, "you're clenching…*so* fucking tight. I'm gonna come."

Me too, I think, but I've lost the ability to speak, concentrating on holding back, instead letting out little "*Ungh, ungh, ungh*"s as we rock together. I'm practically a pretzel at this point, bent in half with my knees near my ears as Dmitri throws his body weight over me to kiss me again without any finesse at all.

I grip at his shoulders, snaking my trembling hands under the jacket, needing to feel skin on skin.

"Come with me, darling boy," he demands, "you've been so good. You can come now. Come for Daddy. Come—*oh, fuck,* just like that. Good boy. Good boy. *Fuuuuuuck.*"

Somewhere in the midst of my convulsing, I realize that he's coming, too, flooding me with warmth and wetness that feels so naughty as he carefully pulls out, given that it trickles out with him.

I snuggle into Dmitri, dimly aware of Jake cutting filming while I fight the heaviness of my eyelids.

He chuckles and gives me a gentle shake. "C'mon, honey, let's go shower."

"Oh, bonus content?" one of the camera guys asks, and Dmitri shakes his head.

"Not today." He glances over at Jake. "How'd we do for timing? Do we need to add to the scene?"

"I don't think we'll need to trim much in editing from what I saw, so I think that's a wrap." Jake grins. "I have a good feeling about this one."

Feeling a bit more awake and alert, my lips quirk. "What will it be called?"

Jake frowns. "The same thing it was going to be called when you were booked for the gig. *Miracle On 69th Street.*"

If I'd known that...

"But we didn't even sixty-nine," I protest. "You don't think people will expect that?"

Jake shrugs. "It's porn, Miles. It's not that complex."

"But…"

"What else would you suggest?" Dmitri cuts in swiftly, laughing, "My suggestion is *Santa's Ho…Ho Ho.* Or, *oooh! Santa's Ho Fo' Sho'.*"

Snorting, Jake and I shoot him down in unison with an emphatic, "*No.*"

Dmitri takes it in stride, swinging his legs off the side of the bed and offering me his hand. "Fine, ignore my genius. But come shower with me, anyway."

It's not an offer I can refuse, especially as a pang of melancholy hits with the realization that our time together is ending and so is the manufactured festive bubble I found myself in.

Oh, sure, the real holiday season is only just around the corner, but for a little while there, I really did lose myself in the fun and fantasy of our Christmas scene…and, somehow, I don't think blasting Mariah Carey on repeat is going to help recapture that.

Still, I need to consider myself lucky. I got to participate in an extended scene with my dream Daddy Dom *and* I'm getting paid for it. The other subs at The Grove are going to be so jealous!

You never know, I muse as Dmitri finally sheds his jacket and adjusts the water temperature before pulling me into the large shower stall with him, *maybe we'll hook up at The Grove again sometime.*

I'm adding that to my Christmas wish list.

Chapter Eight

I should have asked for his number, I sigh, sinking into the plush booth seat of one of the tables lining the outside of The Grove's main club floor. I've turned up every other night for two weeks straight, but I'm yet to catch a glimpse of Miles.

He had been subdued during our shower, and even more so when we'd gotten dressed in our street clothes, but not to the point where I'd worried about sub drop. We'd chatted and he accepted my compliments on how fun it was to work with him with a sweet blush and dip of his chin...and it wasn't until after I'd walked him to his car and watched him carefully back out of the park and drive away that I realized I hadn't asked for his number.

The first sub I have felt a spark of something special with in God-only-knows how long and I let him slip through my fingers.

Now, I know I could call Jake and ask him to shoot me Miles's contact details under the ruse of wanting to talk about work with him, but that would be disingenuous and unprofessional. So, instead, I've been visiting The Grove regularly...which seems mildly stalkerish and possibly a little sad, but somehow that is still better than being unprofessional.

Marginally.

"Who pissed in your Fruit Loops?" a cheerful voice asks, and I turn my head to find Josh Walker sliding into the booth seat across from me.

He's kind of notorious here at The Grove for being a Grade A brat. Such a brat, in fact, that he has *two* Daddy Doms to keep him in line. Young and buff, just like Miles, Josh is not the kind of person you'd assume is a sub at first glance, and you'd never guess that he's also a Little. Especially when you find out that he's a Detective on the local police force.

"*Josh*," one of his Daddies, another cop named Max, warns. I've known Max for years, having been Doms in the same scene together since I landed in town, but I can't say we're close. Still, he smiles easily at me and says, "Sorry, Big D. He's angling for an epic punishment tonight."

Josh just shoots me a cheeky smile and a wink. My heart gives a little pang, unable to ignore how similar this behavior is to Miles's bratting.

Max, being shorter than his Boy, just folds his arms and looms over the table at him. "Say sorry, monkey."

Josh's brown eyes glimmer with humor and I watch the moment Max clocks it and realizes his mistake. But it's too late, Josh is already smirking back and parroting, "Sorry monkey."

I hide my own smile behind my hand, but Max still turns his glare onto me. "Don't encourage him."

"But he's smiling, Daddy," Josh says, sounding particularly proud of himself. "I'm just trying to help."

"We both know you're acting out because Em had to work late with your brother tonight," Max replies. "Just think about how Daddy Em is going to react when I tell him what a pest you're being."

Josh's eyes widen with dawning horror. "Not the cage, Daddy, please. I *hate* wearing the cage."

"That's why it's a punishment, baby. And you've earned at least half an hour of it already. Maybe even while sucking my cock."

"No! No, I'm sorry. I'm *sorry*," he draws the plaintive word out, before turning to me and begging, "I'm sorry I was rude. I just saw that you looked all *grr* and I wanted to cheer you up."

I don't spend a lot of time with Littles, and while Josh isn't the type to regress super young, he's still clearly fallen into headspace. I turn to Max, silently deferring to him. He's Josh's Daddy, after all.

Max sighs. "You had good intentions, monkey, but the delivery needed work. You didn't even ask Dmitri if he was okay with you joining him."

"Shi—*er*—oot. Shoot." Josh bites his lip and gives me a baleful look. "Sorry about that, too."

Damn, but he reminds me of Miles. So willing to please, but with a playful side which needs a firm hand sometimes. Thinking this way makes me softer and more lenient than I would be with any other bratty sub.

"It's fine, Josh," I respond gently, then tilt my chin up towards Max, "but your Daddy's right: with anyone else you might be in big trouble. However," I hope I'm not overstepping, "because I know you're just missing your other Daddy, and I know how grumpy missing someone special makes me, maybe Daddy Max might consider cutting that cage time in half if you promise to be good for the rest of the night."

Max snorts. "Oh, good; another big, tough-ass Dom going soft for him," he teases. "Don't let those puppy eyes fool you, D, or he'll walk all over you."

I'm back to thinking of another sub and his big, round, pleading eyes, and kisses that stole my heart in one fell swoop. "Yeah," I smile, glancing between the pair of them, imagining Josh doing the same thing to his Daddies, "I'd believe that."

Except Max and Emmet, the huge bear of a man who completes their triad, weren't stupid enough to let Josh disappear right under their noses.

When another glance around the dimly lit club space doesn't miraculously produce the Boy I've been hoping to see again, I gesture to the seat across from me. "Sit, Max. Have a drink with me." I tilt my head to the side. "Unless you're doing a scene tonight?" The Grove has a strict sobriety rule for anyone participating in scenes involving bondage, or pain or impact play, among other things. The bar is for people who want to hang out in the nightclub, but for anyone indulging in kinky scenes, it's expected that we stay sober for safety and consent.

"Outside of putting a cage on my naughty Boy, no. But I'm not a big drinker anyway." He pulls out his phone to scan the QR code on the table, which will bring an order directly to our booth. "Still, a beer sounds good." He turns to Josh. "Would you like a soda? Juice in a sippy cup?"

"Soda please, Daddy." All traces of Josh's earlier cheek and sass have been replaced by sweetness.

"Good boy," Max praises.

Watching the answering smile bloom over Josh's face as he revels in the praise, it's hard not to recall just how much Miles loves being told how good he is. How much he so obviously craves it.

Ugh.

I'm starting to think I will have to ask Jake for his contact details after all.

The three of us make small talk while we wait for our drinks to arrive, and it distracts me enough that, even when Max asks how work is going for me, my thoughts don't immediately circle back to Miles. Instead, I talk about the few projects I've been involved in, and answer Josh's carefully worded questions about working in the adult entertainment industry.

I appreciate that neither of them are at all fazed or judgmental about my chosen career, and that Josh has clearly taken Max's instruction to think through his delivery to heart.

"...and I just wrapped a Christmas themed shoot the other week," I finish, shaking my head with a rueful smile. "Tacky puns and all."

"*Please* tell me you were dressed as a badass elf," Josh begs with a laugh. "Or...oh! Instead of puppy play, was there reindeer play?"

"I was a badass Santa, actually," I grin, but I feel my expression fade as Miles's adorable words ("You're *Father* Christmas...and you look like a Daddy.") replay in my mind. Clearing my throat and giving my head a shake, I add, "And no, there wasn't any pet play of any kind."

"Pity," Josh sighs, running his finger around the rim of his now half-empty glass. "Reindeer play sounds like fun." Then, as if a lightbulb has lit up above his head, he straightens and beams at his Daddy.

Max is already a step ahead of him. "Yes," he says in an exaggerated 'you don't even need to ask' kind of tone, "we can try it out. I'm sure Daddy Em will also be happy to let you experiment if you want, monkey."

"You're the best, Daddy Maxxie."

The way Josh stares at Max with hearts in his eyes makes me avert my own. In the next moment, I'm glad that I did, because I catch a glimpse of a familiar face as Miles eases his way around the main club room.

Pushing to my feet, I make my apologies, refusing to take my eyes off Miles in case I lose him in the crowd. But he's wearing a neon-yellow safety vest, so I hardly think that's going to be an issue.

Dimly aware of Max and Josh saying goodbye, I hurry after my sub.

This time, if nothing else, I am getting his number.

Chapter Nine

I t feels weird to be walking through The Grove in my work clothes. But, seeing as I'm actually here to work, I can't wear one of my usual club outfits.

See, when I'm not trying to get my big break on the silver screen (or, apparently, *any* screen now), I'm an electrician, and I work for the company that designed, installed, and maintains the entire intricate security system here at The Grove. And, because they liked those services so much, we soon took over all of their electrical needs.

But, due to the nature of their business, we also need to have technicians available twenty-four-seven in case of any urgent issues, and we're all on a rotating roster to provide that support. Ninety percent of the time, callouts happen during the day. It's just my luck that they discovered a sparking light switch in one of the upstairs theme rooms during my 'on call' days.

Never mind that it was a similar callout which introduced me to the delights of the club almost two years ago now; I've been doing my best to keep my distance the past couple of weeks. It's been torture, but I knew that if I saw Dmitri with any of the other subs, it might just break my heart.

And how ridiculous is that?

We're not dating. We're not even regular scene partners. He's not my Dom or my Daddy. He's just a really amazing guy who gave me an absolutely mind-blowing experience on a porn set, of all places.

I barely spent two hours with him, so there's no reason I should feel so attached.

But the heart wants what it wants.

So, to try and wean myself out of the *way too strong* feelings I developed during our scenes together, I've been staying away from The Grove.

Until tonight.

Meg waved me on through to the main club space and I skirted around the edges, aiming for the side hallway that leads to the elevators and grand staircase at the back of the building. On the outside, this whole place just looks like one giant industrial shed. But on the inside, it's damn near magical.

Split into two stories, downstairs is a huge nightclub, with parallel hallways bracketing the club space, each with their own locker rooms and bathrooms. They meet around the back of the club area in a U shape, where two elevators frame a lush, red carpeted staircase.

Like the security system, the soundproofing in this place is next level, because when you make it upstairs to the hallways that look like something out of a swanky hotel, you can't hear the music from downstairs at all. It's a different world up here.

Each hallway has half a dozen doors, which lead to themed rooms for hire. There's everything from upscale offices, a classroom, and even a well-stocked dungeon along here. At the far end of the hallway, a massive age regression playroom takes up at least a third of the upstairs space, running from one side of the building to the other. I don't partake in age play, but even I get excited any time I'm in that big room...mostly because of the inviting bouncy castle nestled at the far end of the space. It's hard not to see the appeal in that.

But tonight I'm headed for one of the rooms designed to resemble the inside of a rustic log cabin, and I fish the key from my back pocket when I get there. And *that's* when I clock movement out of the corner of my eye. My breath catches when I register who is walking towards me.

"I'm not stalking you," Dmitri jokes, smiling that same damn smile that makes my stomach flip. Then he sees the keycard in my hand —outstretched towards the reader above the handle— and I take an unreasonable amount of pleasure out of the way his expression briefly flickers into disappointment before it smooths into an approximation of apology. "Sorry, you're meeting someone?"

It sounds like he's fishing for information and, damn it, but I love that. I want to believe that he was just as affected by our short time together as I was.

"No," I shake my head, "I'm working, actually." I gesture to my shirt in response to the adorable crinkle in his brow. "My day job. I'm an electrician. They've reported a fault in this room and it's not safe for anyone to use the lights or sockets in here until I've fixed it."

And it is super awesome that the club sprung to have every room on its own little circuit, too, though I think they realized that it's easier to shut down one room than an entire building if anything goes wrong. Like tonight, for example.

"Oh!" All right, that is *definitely* relief I hear in his voice, and I can see it in the way his shoulders loosen and his smile seems less forced and more...well, *Dmitri*. "That's cool. I bet you have heaps of buddies asking you to come help around their places, huh?"

"I get bribed with pizza and beer occasionally, yeah," I chuckle, and finally lift the card to the reader on the door. It beeps and a little green light above the handle lets me know I've successfully unlocked it, so I press the handle down and push the door open.

Dmitri reaches towards the switch on the wall.

"Don't!" I grab his wrist. Jolts of electricity which have *nothing* to do with the faulty circuit in the room skitter up my arm. "Faulty wiring, remember?"

His eyes widen. "Shit, sorry. Force of habit."

I nod. "I get it." Really, I should be insisting that he waits outside, but I'm too selfish and I've been missing him too much to do that. I gesture to the couch, a plush black leather monstrosity set in front of a fake fireplace, with a large faux fur rug on the floor between them. "Go sit. This won't take me too long."

He does as he's told while I locate the room's electrical panel, stealthily concealed behind a framed tapestry of a forest scene. He's quiet while I do my thing, trying to see if the issue is just a blown circuit or whether there's any faulty wiring at play. The spark might also have been caused by a buildup of carbon in the switch, but my money is on a bad wire, given that it happened a couple of times before they called us.

For a handful of minutes, he's quiet, letting me concentrate on my job. I find the bad wire easily enough, and start my mental checklist on repairing it.

"I should have asked for your number." Dmitri's voice cuts into my thoughts, and my brain grinds to a halt.

Turning to face him, I find him leaning against the armrest of the leather lounge, his gaze sharp and pinned on me. My heart skips a beat. "Yeah?"

"Yeah," he agrees. "I thought we had chemistry, and I had a lot of fun doing those scenes with you."

I'm barely able to process what he's saying, too distracted by how good he looks in his molded-on jeans and a black t-shirt that clings to his biceps then drapes over his soft belly in the most delicious way possible.

I'd thought he was hot dressed as Sexy Santa, but this casual Daddy energy is something else entirely. I want to throw myself over his lap and accept my punishment for avoiding him...not that he knows that I was.

"Is that okay?" he asks when I'm quiet for too long.

"Hmm?"

"That I enjoyed our scenes and was hoping to connect outside of work."

"No," I shake my head, then cringe. "I mean *yes*, it's okay. It's more than okay. I wanted that, too. I just thought..." I trail off, unable to verbalize how I'd felt when we parted ways after our shoot.

I'd been the brattiest I'd ever been, when I'd wanted to prove what a good sub I am. I felt like maybe I was too much work, that I can't follow instructions, and that I'd blown any chance at having a private repeat session with him, let alone anything more.

His eyes bore into mine, his expression and tone serious as he prods, "You thought?"

"I...should get back to work." I turn back to the electrical panel with my heart in my throat and my thoughts all jumbled.

"Miles."

Oh, God, that voice...

Shaking my head, I start to isolate the faulty section of wiring from the rest. I open my mouth to tell him that we will talk, but that I need to concentrate first, but the horror of my own mistake hits me moments before the pain registers.

I never de-energized the system.

I'm wearing rubber-soled shoes, but the shock to the system still reverberates through me, making me fall backwards. Dimly, I hear Dmitri call out, but I surrender to darkness before I even hit the floor.

Chapter Ten

I refuse to leave Miles's side over the course of the next few hours, only stepping back when the paramedics arrive, but then I demand to travel in the ambulance with them. In the Emergency Department, the attending doctor, an attractive blonde guy whose name tag reads 'Doctor Anson Meyers', seems to recognize Miles, who is still drifting in and out of consciousness.

Before I can get jealous and possessive, though, he turns to me and says, "If you sit down and stay quiet while I work, you can stay. My Daddy would lose his shit if something like that happened to me and he had to be separated from me."

Nodding and swallowing roughly, all I can manage is a gruff, "Thank you."

It's hard to sit in the corner and listen as the doctor calmly discusses things like watching for any signs of an erratic pulse with the nurse at his side. They hook Miles up to various monitors, and I bite my lip when they start talking about possible nerve damage when it becomes obvious that some of Miles's muscles are spasming.

I was feeling guilty enough for distracting him, for essentially causing his accident, but if there's permanent damage...

"You said the contact with the live wire was only short?" the doctor's voice pulls me out of my spiral. I swallow roughly.

"Yeah," I bob my head once, my gaze drifting away from the doctor's blue eyes to settle back on Miles's twitching form, "it was a split second. He cried out and fell back and hit the ground before I was even up out of my seat." I'm worried about how hard his head hit the floor, too, now that I think about it.

"And he's regained consciousness?"

"He's been in and out since it happened, yeah."

"Was he able to focus when he was awake?"

"I don't know. The paramedics said it was a good sign."

It's times like this where I feel so inadequate as a grown-ass man. All of these people are so much more educated than I am and I can barely string together two sentences. What if I miss telling them something important? Something that could help Miles?

Doctor Meyers inclines his head. "Yes, I've read his chart. But sometimes a partner just knows when something isn't right."

I blink, my heart sinking. "Oh." Clearing my throat, I move to add, "I'm not—"

"D'ddy?" Miles's slurring cuts me off, and my heart races to hear it. I lean forward, reaching for him, even as the doctor spins quickly to smile at Miles in greeting.

"The room might seem a bit bright, Miles, so be careful opening your eyes, okay?"

Miles's handsome face contorts into a frown of confusion, and he starts to squint. "Daddy?"

The nurse assisting the doctor barely blinks when the blonde man waves a hand in my direction, despite Miles not being able to see it. "He's here. You're okay. You just had a bit of an ordeal, so we need to check you out."

Miles lets out a whine of discontentment, and seems to strain a little to focus through his squinted vision. "Anson?"

The doctor beams at him, nodding. "The one and only. That's a great sign for your memory being intact. I think we've only met a few times in passing."

"Wh'h'ppned?" Miles goes back to barely managing to articulate his words, but the doctor doesn't seem fazed.

Pulling out a penlight, he leans over the bed and gently lifts Miles's left eyelid, peering into the eye before repeating the process on the right, nodding when Miles flinches. "What do you remember?"

Miles closes his eyes and the frown he's wearing deepens. "W'rk." He pauses, then cracks his eyes open, seemingly forcing himself to speak clearly, talking slowly and with significant effort, "Dmitri was there."

"That's excellent, Miles," the doctor smiles again. "Anything else?"

Miles gives it a moment before shaking his head, then grimacing.

"Headache?" asks the doctor.

"Uh-huh." Miles scrunches his eyes shut. "Wh're'm'I?"

"You're in the hospital," the doctor answers in the same calm, genial tone he's been using since we were rushed in here. "You touched a live wire and, for lack of a better term, were electrocuted. The force from the electricity and the pain threw you back, and you hit your head when you fell. You've been in and out of consciousness for a little while, but this is the first you've been lucid since the accident."

Miles winces again. "Shit. I forgot..." He gives his head another shake, this one slower than the last. "'M in trouble."

"With who?" prods the doctor.

"M'boss," Miles sighs.

"Accidents like this happen to even the most seasoned professionals," the doctor assures him. "Your boss is probably going to be more concerned about your recovery than any mistakes you may have made."

Miles deflates, seeming to slump even further into the flimsy hospital pillow. His eyelids droop, and the doctor peppers him with a few more questions, then explains he's also being monitored for a concussion.

"You'll be kept in for at least twenty-four hours for observation," the doctor finally explains, "because we're especially concerned about your body spasms and twitching. It could just be residual trauma from the shock, but if it continues, I'd like to check for nerve damage. Your only job right now is to rest and not think too hard, okay? Very minimal screen time for the next forty-eight hours, and then we can talk about reintroducing some light, non-strenuous movement into your routine."

Miles frowns. "But...work?" Even though he looks tired, he's more alert, and isn't slurring his speech as much. Even I know that's a good sign.

"Ideally, I think you need to take at least a week off to recover. And I'd like it if you had someone with you monitoring you for that time, too. Just in case there are any complications from the electrocution that we've missed."

"I don't really have anyone who—"

Miles starts, but I interrupt with, "You've got me."

He startles, then winces, but still sits up a bit straighter, squinting and scanning the room until his gaze lands on me. A billion micro expressions flit over his handsome face in the span of a few seconds, everything from relief to disbelief to guilt. "You don't have to."

Even if I wasn't feeling guilty for causing his distraction and landing him here in the first place, I would be saying the same thing. "Darling boy, I *want* to."

He bites his lip, his cheeks dusting a pretty pink color. "Okay."

And that's that.

Chapter Eleven

"**S**o…this is your place," I say with a hint of curiosity as Dmitri helps me out of the passenger seat of his car. He has been practically glued to my side since the accident, only leaving the hospital when the nurses kicked him out for overstaying visiting hours.

Dmitri lives in a cozy little cottage-style home, it seems. With its white picket fence, steep, gabled roof, and inviting porch (complete with two white rocking chairs), I never would have guessed that this big, burly, tattooed man lives here.

Then again, he's one of the sweetest people I've ever met, so maybe it does fit him.

"Home sweet home," he acknowledges with a smile, then reaches to unlatch the front gate. He presses his palm into the small of my back and guides me up the cobblestone path, letting the gate shut behind us. "Just be careful of Juniper. She doesn't realize how big she is and she gets excited sometimes."

I frown. "Who's—"

A deep, loud bark sounds from the other side of the front door, cutting me off.

"That's Junie," he answers my unfinished question fondly, then slides his key into the lock. Before he turns it, though, he pauses. "You're okay with dogs, right? Not allergic or afraid of them?"

"I love dogs," I grin back, feeling my heart flutter when his concern melts into a relieved smile of his own. "But I can't have one in my little studio apartment."

"Thank god," he breathes, finally turning the key. "I should have asked before bringing you here. I didn't even think until now."

"You don't have to have me stay here. I'm fine. I can just get a cab home and—"

"Nope. The doctor said you shouldn't be alone and, honestly, I would worry too much if I thought you were."

"You know you're not responsible for—*oh my god.* That's a *horse,* not a dog." He's swung the door open and the big, black and white animal tippy-tapping her feet on the polished wooden floors is one hundred percent the size of a small pony.

Dmitri drops my bag to the floor with a *thud* and reaches out to rub the now whining horse-dog between the ears. She leans into him, resting her head above his belly button and I watch as he actively braces himself against her weight.

"Junie, this is Miles," he says, introducing me to the one-headed Cerberus. "We need to be calm and gentle around Miles right now, all right? No bowling him over or climbing into his lap on the couch."

She whines up at him, pleading with giant brown eyes.

"Gentle," he repeats.

Juniper seems to sigh and then rolls those big eyes my way. I have to admit, she is absolutely gorgeous, with drooping jowls and the most pitiful expression I've ever seen on a dog. Her tail gives a short, cautious wag, and I reach out a hand for her to sniff. The wagging picks up once she's decided I'm not a threat.

"Junie," Dmitri uses his firm Daddy voice as she steps towards me, "*gentle*, remember?"

"She's fine," I assure him, then almost regret it when the Great Dane sits on my foot and then leans her whole body into my side, snuffling up at me and whimpering until I pet her like Dmitri was only a few seconds ago.

I must wobble a little, because Dmitri's hand is immediately steadying me again, and he says, "Let's go into the living room and get you comfortable. The doctor said you should take it easy for the next couple of days, remember?"

Junie's paws patter behind us as he ushers me into the room to our left, guiding me down onto a plush, dark brown couch. Juniper leaps up on the seat beside me, then flops without any grace, landing her oversized head in my lap.

Dmitri sighs and gives her the side-eye. "Well, at least she's not sitting *on* you."

"She's being gentle like you asked," I agree, rumpling the soft skin between her ears, making them flop back and forth. "She's being good." An involuntary flush of heat rushes over my cheeks, my own words making me remember how amazing it felt being told that *I* was being good for him. Before I know it, my mouth has overridden my brain and I'm blurting, "When you said you wanted..." I don't finish the sentence, unable to really remember what he'd said the other night. It's all a bit fuzzy.

He frowns, probably just as lost with my train of thought as I am. Dropping to a crouch in front of me, he squeezes my knee, "When I said I wanted to spend more time with you outside of work?"

"Work?" I tilt my head carefully to the side. I'm still wary of setting off more headaches.

"The adult film shoot."

Oh.

I know I was paid for it, but is it wrong that I didn't think of it as work? I enjoyed it, for one, and for another thing... "I was there by accident."

Dmitri's jaw drops at my unplanned confession. "Pardon?"

Grimacing, I explain, "I was supposed to be auditioning for some Hallmark-esque Christmas movie, but I later found out that my agent sent me the wrong studio details" —he had switched my shoot with his other new starter's, it turned out— "and I...um...well, once I worked out what was happening, I stayed."

I'm a little concerned that I've broken him. His mouth moves, but no sound comes out.

"Dmitri?"

Holding up an index finger, his tone is strained when he finally replies, "Let me get this straight. You had no idea you were walking into a porn shoot and once you got there you just" —he rolls his wrist— "went with it."

"Well, yeah. I, uh, I thought...y'know...why not? How different could it be to doing scenes at The Grove?" I dig my fingers into the fur of Junie's rough, letting her warmth keep me calm as my heart races. "Is that...is that bad?"

Dmitri's eyes widen and he shakes his head quickly, pushing up from the floor to sit beside me, perched awkwardly on the armrest of the couch. He wraps his arm around my shoulders and squeezes. "No, of course it's not bad, baby. I just wasn't expecting to hear that. You were a natural. Jake says the finished product is one of the best shoots he's seen all year. And to hear that you went into it on a *whim* is just...wow."

With my shoulders inching up to my ears, I repeat, "It was like doing a scene for an audience at The Grove."

And I liked it.

Fuck that, I *loved* it.

But how much of that was because I was already half-infatuated with my scene partner?

"Would you do it again?" he asks.

I have a ready answer for this question, having thought those very same words over and over again at least three times a day since we filmed it. But to give Dmitri my answer out loud is scary, because it's going to give away more than I think he's ready to hear.

"Miles?" he prods gently. "It's okay if you—"

"Only with you."

Jesus. Is it the pain meds making me lose control of my mouth today?

Dmitri's arm tenses around me and I have to close my eyes against the rejection I know is coming.

"Precious, look at me."

Trying to hide how rapidly my heart is racing, I focus on keeping my breathing calm as I turn to face him, barely able to look him in the eye.

"Can you tell me why you'd only do it again with me?" I can't read his tone properly, but am I imagining the hint of hope in it?

At this point, I don't have anything left to lose by being honest. My dignity and sense of self-preservation have already disappeared. Besides, Christmas is coming up, after all, and if I had just one wish? It would be to make our Santa Daddy fantasy real for life.

So, I take a deep breath and tell him, "Because I only want you to be my Daddy, Dmitri. At the club, on screen, at home…I only want it to be you." And there it is. I can't make my feelings any plainer. *Oh.* Except for one more thing. "And I know that filming is your job, and I'm not asking you to stop working with other actors for me. But…I kind of want to be the only Boy who calls you Daddy."

There's barely a moment for me to worry that I might have said too much, or crossed a line in asking such a thing of him, before he's holding my face between his big, tattooed hands and pressing his lips to mine with a sense of urgency that I can feel deep in my own bones.

My lips part for him, letting him in, breathing in the spicy scent of his beard-oil and cologne. His kiss is just as perfect as I remember, only now it feels like so much more. There's no audience, unless you count the dog. No cameras. Nothing demanding this of us. It's natural, organic, and *real.*

"I want all of that, too, Miles," he whispers when the kiss draws to an end, but he doesn't pull away. His breath washes over me, just as minty as he tasted, warm and strangely comforting. "I've been kicking myself since I let you drive away without asking for your number. We barely know each other, but that scene with you…we clicked in a way I've never experienced before. I want to be your Daddy. On screen, at the club, at home. Every way you'll have me. It's too early to know what the future holds, but…" he presses his forehead to mine and stares into my eyes, making my stomach swoop, "I have a good feeling about it."

"Yeah," I manage to rasp out, finding his smile and optimism contagious, "me, too."

"**H**oly shit, Big D," Jake chortles down the line, "you *have got* to see the comments rolling in on *Miracle*."

I put my phone on speaker and smile widely at Miles, where he pauses, crouched over the box of Christmas decorations I'd pulled down from the attic at his begging.

"Well, I've got Miles here with me," I tell Jake, "and you're on speaker. Go nuts."

"Oh, *do you*?" The teasing lilt in my old friend's voice has me rolling my eyes. "I knew you two had chemistry. Would you consider letting me and the boys come and shoot some additional scenes at your place?"

"I'm *up* for it," Miles leers at me, and I snort.

"Behave, precious. You know what happens when you tease Daddy."

"Uh, guys, I'm still here." Jake laughs. "But, seriously, people *love* you. They're begging for an encore. *Oh*, maybe we could do a Valentine's themed follow-up?"

"I'm *not* dressing as sexy cupid," I warn him.

"But I might," Miles says. "Tighty-whities and a bow and arrow? I could rock it."

"Sold!" Jake cries before I can nix the idea, kind of wanting to keep that level of sexiness all to myself. "Start thinking up Valentine's puns, guys. The comedy with the sex and the heart...it's *pure gold.*"

Giving me a cheeky smirk, Miles taps his plump lower lip with his index finger as he improvises, "Hmmm...Roses are red, violets are blue, I'll get on my knees 'cos I know what to do."

Jake sounds beyond impressed. "Yes! Save that energy for the cameras."

I watch as my boyfriend gears up to say something else, likely even cheekier, and I can't take a moment more being cockblocked by my friend and sometimes colleague. "Sure thing, Jake. Sounds like a plan. Anyway, we're putting up the tree—"

"*Now?*" Jake sounds scandalized. "It's Christmas Eve! You waited until Christmas Eve to put up your tree? What kind of—"

"Bye, Jake, Merry Christmas!" I cut him off and end the call, never taking my eyes off my Boy.

The past couple of months have been wonderful. Miles slipped into my daily life almost like he's always been here. I am convinced that Junie loves him more than she loves me now, and with the way he sneaks her dog-safe treats from his plate whenever we're eating a meal and he thinks I'm not looking, I'm convinced he has bribed her to achieve that top spot. But I can't be mad about it. I think it's awesome that he loves my baby as much as I do.

And then there's the fact that everything we do together just feels easy. He keeps me on my toes for sure, but I love almost every minute of it. Yeah, there's been some adjustment having him stay over more often than not —he leaves his wet towels on the bathroom floor, and he hates that I don't rinse my dishes before I put them in the dishwasher— but those teething pains are worth it for the sheer joy I feel having him in my home and in my life in general.

Before we met, I was in a rut. I was bored with monotony, and tired of doing the same scenes day in and day out. I enjoyed being a Dom, but even that had been getting old, with doting subs who never challenged me, and who never made me think outside the box.

Then along came Miles, with his cheeky grin and silly puns, and he was like a breath of fresh air. He's bratty but desperate for praise. He wants me to himself but gets off on performing for others. He hates feeling embarrassed but loves to be humiliated sexually. He's gorgeous, funny, and sweet. My perfect, darling boy.

And I love him.

I think I've loved him since the first time he called me Daddy. It would have been crazy to think it back then, but those besotted feelings have only grown into deeper, more serious ones.

I'm also pretty sure he feels the same way.

There's only one way to be certain, and is there a better time than Christmas Eve? Especially considering how we met?

"What's that look for, Daddy?" he asks with a knowing smirk. "I thought I was being good giving Jake what he asked us for."

Oh, this boy...

"You were trying to get a rise out of me," I answer, choosing my words deliberately, knowing that he won't be able to help himself.

Sure enough, he abandons the box of decorations and stalks towards me, grinning widely. "I do love making certain parts of you rise, yes."

From her position napping next to the box, Junie raises her head to track Miles's movements, then flops back down with a huff. Unless food is involved, she's not likely to move again for a while.

"Are you being naughty, darling?" I ask, grabbing Miles and tugging him down into my lap where he squirms deliciously, then gasps when he discovers how hard I already am for him.

"*Daddy...*" he grinds his hips, and it's all I can do to not give into temptation yet.

"Uh-uh," I scold gently, "we're still talking."

"I've forgotten what we were talking about," he admits, sounding a bit breathy. "It's hard to think when I know you're hard and ready to go."

I can definitely relate to that.

Nevertheless...

"Try for me, precious. We were talking about you being cheeky to get a reaction out of me. Are you angling for a spanking tonight?"

Miles's breathing quickens and I hear him gulp, but he shakes his head. "Not really."

"No? Even though that's what Santa Daddy gave naughty Miles in our video?"

We watched the finished product together before Jake posted it at the beginning of December, and we've talked about role-playing and reliving it, seeing as we enjoyed it so much. Doing it at Christmas, specifically, sounded like it would be a lot of fun.

"I never got to suck Santa's candy-cane," he pouts. "I want to do that this time."

"And you can't do that if I spank you?"

He shakes his head, then dips his chin, turning his face fully away so I can't see him. That won't do at all.

Moving him off my lap and onto the seat beside me, I use my Daddy voice, "*Miles.*"

"I'll come," he whines. "I *always* come when you spank me. It's like...like a Pavlovian response to it now. Like you've trained my body to come when you spank me."

It's difficult to hold back my chuckle, but somehow I manage. It's probably the fact that he sounds genuinely bereaved. Instead, I stroke his back. "I love that you make a mess every time I make your perfect ass cheeks glow, baby. You know that."

"Yeah, but Santa's rule was no coming. And if I come, I don't get to suck Santa's cock."

"Oh, I see. Well, what if Santa changes his rules this time?"

His throat works for a moment. "Why would Santa Daddy do that?"

"Because it's Christmas, precious. And," I pause to make sure I have his complete attention, gazing into his beautiful eyes as I add, "I love you, Miles."

Joy lights up his features even while his eyes well with tears. "Oh my God," he murmurs in awe, and I don't know whether he meant to say it out loud or not. Then he swallows again and says, "I love you, too, Dmitri. So much."

"Even if I make you come every time I spank you?"

His resulting laughter is watery, but he's nodding. "Yes," he leans in, dropping his voice lower, as if sharing a secret, "maybe *especially* because of that."

With his mouth so close to mine, I can't resist the temptation to dip down and claim it with my own. I start with good intentions, kissing him sweetly after our shared feelings, but then he climbs back into my lap, straddling me, and all bets are off.

I moan when he grinds down, his erection bumping against my own. All plans to get into costume and reprise our silly sexy Christmas roles vanish, swept from my mind at the touch of his tongue against mine and the sound of his needy mewls and whines.

I lose myself in him, in his soft sighs and in the way his fingers tug at the ends of the longer hair on the top of my head. The way his mouth tastes like sugar cookies, and the hard press of his abs against my softer belly. This kiss is all heat and affection; a celebration of our feelings for each other and a filthy promise of things to come.

Speaking of things to come...

Miles eventually draws back to breathe, and gives me a saucy wink. "Hey, Daddy?"

The glint in his eye makes my dick twitch with anticipation. It's the same glint that I saw on the day we met, the one that promises his cheeky, slightly bratty side is about to come out to play. And, God, but I love that side of him. I love every side of him.

"...Yes?" I stretch the word out with exaggerated caution, playing his game, knowing it's what he wants from me in this moment.

His kiss-swollen lips stretch wide, and for a second I'm distracted, already imagining them wrapped around my aching cock. But then he speaks, "Did you know that we're like hot chocolate and marshmallows?"

Oh, no. Does this count as a Christmas pun?

I thought we were done with these.

Still, he's practically vibrating on my lap, so I sigh and give in. "How's that, precious?"

"Well, you're hot...and I want to be on top of you."

I snort and groan all at once, affecting exaggerated disgust, "That one was *awful*, baby."

Miles pouts. "So...you *don't* want me on top of you?"

I grip his hips and thrust up against him, letting him feel just how much I definitely don't hate the idea. "Now, I never said that," I drawl, watching his eyelashes flutter shut and grinning at the damp spot forming at the front of his gray sweats, "but I thought Daddy's good boy wanted to suck Santa's candy cane?"

Instead of a verbal response, Miles clamors off my lap, landing on the rug on his knees with a dull *thump*. I spread my legs further apart in invitation, chuckling at his enthusiasm to pull my erection out of my own sweatpants, lifting my hips to give him better access as he tugs my pants down my thighs.

My cock, much like I'm sure his is, is already wet and throbbing with need. It strains up towards my belly, flushed and purpled at the head.

On his best behavior tonight, Miles wraps his fingers around the base, but looks up at me and asks, "Can I suck it now, Daddy?" in his most submissive voice.

"Fuck, yes, precious."

He doesn't wait another second, lapping at the head before taking the entire length to the back of his throat.

The first time he'd demonstrated this ability, I'd nearly gone cross-eyed at the pleasure. The hot, wet heat. The suction. The feeling of those plump lips stretched wide around the base of my shaft, brushing my balls...

Even after months of experiencing this perfection, it's still almost overwhelming. Especially when he swallows and I can feel his throat constricting around the head of my dick.

"*Yes,* baby. Fuck, your mouth is so perfect."

He makes a pleased sound that vibrates all the way through me before he begins his slow tease of sucking his way back up the shaft, licking around the head and then diving back down again.

"You're such a good boy for Daddy, Miles. You're doing so good. Just like that. God, I love the way you suck me."

The sounds he's making now are increasing with his own need, and I know that if I don't want him to come in his pants, I need to stop praising him, but I just can't. I have to shower him with dirty praise and compliments, because he's earning it all. He *is* my good boy.

Glancing down my body, I just about come myself when I realize he's staring up at me intently, my cock sliding in and out of those shiny, plump lips as he does. Then I notice that his arm is moving.

"You'd —*ungh*— you'd better not be touching yourself, baby," I warn him. "Daddy wants to watch you come this time."

His eyebrows furrow together, and he whines a little around my dick, but his arm stops moving and, instead, his spare hand reaches up to fondle my balls.

"*Fuck*," I growl out, "that's it. Good boy. God, yes."

At some point, I start to thrust my hips in time with the bobbing motion of his head, reveling in his slurps and occasional gagging sounds. I have to close my eyes to try and stave off the inevitable end as my orgasm rushes closer and closer to the surface.

Soon enough, though, I reach the point of no return.

"Do you want to swallow, precious? Or do you want Daddy to paint your pretty face tonight?"

He whines again, and this time he would definitely be pouting if his mouth wasn't otherwise occupied.

"You...*ohhh, your mouth*...you want Daddy to choose?"

He nods as best he can, glazed, watering eyes staring back at me with adoration.

It's that which does me in. The complete, blinding love in those eyes. I hope he never stops looking at me that way. Especially when he's wrapped around my cock like this.

"Fuck, baby. Fuck." I groan, tensing as my body jerks and my cock swells and pulses down his throat. "Swallow it all down for Daddy."

Miles does just that, finally closing his eyes as he takes every drop I give him. He swallows and sucks until it's too much for my overly sensitized dick to handle, and then he carefully pulls off, licking his lips with satisfaction while I collapse against the back of the couch, my head spinning.

Being the good sub he is, he stays kneeling between my spread thighs, waiting patiently for me to come back to consciousness. I card my fingers into his hair, then slide my hand further down his face, cupping his cheek reverently. He rubs his face into my palm the same way a cat —or Juniper— would. I'm willing to bet that if he could purr, that's what he'd be doing.

"Good boy," I rasp, still catching my breath.

He grins. "So..." he bats his lashes, "does that mean I'm not on Santa's naughty list this year? Because I'd *really* like to come now." After a beat he adds, "Please?"

Patting my thigh, I smirk. "I think it's time for this good boy to sit in Santa's lap and tell him exactly what he wants for Christmas, hmm?"

He scrambles to follow the instruction, straddling me instead of sitting sideways on my knee. With his wrists looped behind my neck, he plants a deep, passionate kiss on my lips, letting me taste myself in his mouth, before he pulls back and declares, "I'd like orgasms, Santa Daddy. Many, many orgasms." We laugh together, and then his voice turns softer and more vulnerable. "But I'd also like to keep you —to keep this, *us*— forever."

"Well, we'd better tell the elves to get the word out, huh?"

Confusion has him scrunching his nose. "Wha—?"

I lean in, whispering conspiratorially, "Because Santa's definitely coming more than once a year from now on until forever."

Miles sputters. "That was *my* pun! I've already used it."

I shrug and nuzzle his nose with mine. "If we're gonna be together forever, baby, we'll have to get used to sharing. What's mine is yours and what's yours is mine, ridiculous puns and all."

He brightens with obvious delight and then squirms, the corner of his lips lifting in that cheeky way which never fails to make my dick twitch with interest. "Then can you hurry up and share those orgasms?"

I arch an eyebrow.

He bats his lashes again. "Please, Santa Daddy? As my Christmas present?"

And, just like when we first met, I can't deny him a thing.

"Only because you're my good boy, darling."

"Always?" his voice is breathy again, eyes fluttering shut with anticipation as my hand creeps between us, rubbing the bulge in his sweats.

"Always and forever, Miles. That's my promise as Santa...and as Daddy."

THE END.

Thank you so much for reading *Dmitri's Darling*. This is Book 3 in my *Kinks & Conundrums* series, and connected to the *Littles & Lace* universe.

If you enjoyed this sweet, fluffy Daddy kink novella, which also functions as a spin off from my *Littles & Lace* series, you may also enjoy *Charlie's Contentment* — a 10,000 word age play novella set in the original *Littles & Lace* series. Currently, you can read *Charlie's Contentment* for free by signing up to my newsletter at:

https://annasparrows.com/newsletter-subscription/

Also, if you would consider leaving a rating or a review for *Dmitri's Darling*, I would be greatly appreciative. Ratings and reviews tell the algorithms which books to share, but they also help me continue to hone my skills as an author.

Thanks again for reading!

Love,

Anna

About the Author

I am a bi Aussie author living in Brisbane, Australia. I've been writing* for as long as I can remember. I started with silly short stories as a kid, moved on to fanfiction in my teens, and then to publishing original fiction in my thirties.

I have been an avid reader of MM romance my whole life. (Ask me about my beginnings with *Buffy* fanfic, haha!) I wrote a sweet and kinky MM romance novel in 2022 and the reader response changed my life. From there, I knew I had found my niche.

And thus Anna Sparrows was born.

*All of my writing is 100% my own. No part of it is generated by Artificial Intelligence (AI) software of any kind. Yes, that means that it's sometimes flawed, but I'm okay with that.

Follow Me

Website: https://annasparrows.com

Facebook: https://www.facebook.com/AnnaSparrowsAuthor

Instagram: https://www.instagram.com/annasparrows

Newsletter: https://annasparrows.com/newsletter-subscription

Also by Anna Sparrows

I write ridiculously sweet & steamy MM romance with guaranteed HEAs…and sometimes with a side of kink. My backlist can be found at annasparrows.com

Dads & Adages Series

Visit Australia's sunny Gold Coast where an assortment of single dads find love and even learn a few life lessons along the way.

Book 1: Where There's A Will

Book 2: You Don't Know Jack

Book 3: A Match Made In Evan

Book 4: Speak Of The Neville (release TBA)

Related: A Surprise For The Holidays

Written in 3rd person POV, *A Surprise for the Holidays* is a sweet, fluffy MM Christmas novella with a grumpy former soccer player turned coach, a golden retriever younger player, and a precocious little girl. Featuring an Aussie Christmas, grumpy/sunshine vibes, an age gap and sand where you're used to snow, this novella brings additional heat to the festive season in more ways than one!

Down Under Daddies Series

Set in rural Western Australia, come meet the and the kinkiest and queerest band of stationhands any outback cattle station has ever seen.

Book 1: A Stable Daddy

Littles & Lace Series

The Littles & Lace series is an MM Age Play series, following a group of like-minded friends in the BDSM community. You'll find mild ABDL, light Pet Play, Femme Play and more here.

Book 1: Asher's Answer

Book 2: Matteo's Mettle

Book 3: Ted's Temerity

Book 4: Spencer's Satisfaction

Book 5: Chance's Choice

Book 6: Josh's Jackpot

Shifters Sanctuary Series

In a world where alphas are thought to be extinct, a number of men are about to have their worlds rocked.

Book 1: His Alpha Unlocked

Book 2: His Prodigal Alpha

Book 3: His Unicorn Alpha

Book 4: His Dragon Duo (TBA)

Kinks & Conundrums Series

A spin-off from the Littles & Lace series, this series follows Daddies, Doms, Littles, and Pet Players as they discover their kinks and find love.

Book 0.5: Baron's Boo-Boo

Book 1: Anson's Awakening

Book 2: Rowan's Renewal

Book 3: Dmitri's Darling

Co-Written With MJ Booth

Completely Pucked (an MM hockey age play romance)

Standalone

Silver (Fox) Linings – A Dad's Best Friend Valentine's Day Novella